Mighty Boy

Mighty Boy

Carol Sonenklar

Orchard Books
New York

Orchard Books
A Grolier Company
95 Madison Avenue
New York, NY 10016

Manufactured in the United States of America
Book design by Vicki Fischman
The text of this book is set in 12 point Souvenir.
1 3 5 7 9 10 8 6 4 2

Library of Congress Cataloging-in-Publication Data
Sonenklar, Carol.
Mighty Boy / by Carol Sonenklar.
p. cm.
Summary: When he gets a chance to meet his hero, the television
character Mighty Boy, Howard Weinstein discovers his own strengths
that help him handle the bully in his new fourth-grade class.
ISBN 0-531-30203-2 (trade : alk. paper).
ISBN 0-531-33203-9 (lib. bdg. : alk. paper)
[1. Self-confidence—Fiction. 2. Bullies—Fiction.] I. Title.
PZ7.S6977Mi 1999
[Fic]—dc21   99-11706

Acknowledgments

Many thanks to my nature experts:
Jim Casselberry, Joe Harding, and the staff at Shaver's Creek Environmental Center at Penn State University

To my two mighty brothers,
Neil and Howard

Mighty Boy

*D*eep in his underground kitchen, surround-
ed by vats of boiling chemicals, Chef
Toxic dipped a fat finger into a pot and
looked thoughtful. "Hmm. I'd say it needs a
pinch of . . . sulfuric acid."

Hearing this, a blond woman in a lab coat,
tied up in the corner of the room, made angry
sounds through the handkerchief stuffed in her
mouth. Chef Toxic threw back his head, almost
knocking off his tall white chef's hat, and
roared with laughter. "What, Miss Flufferbrain?
You have a different recipe? Well, I'm sorry,
my dear, we've already printed up the menus
for today!"

Miss Flufferbrain looked at the calendar on
the wall: today—April 24, 1965—would be the
last day of human civilization. In fifteen seconds, millions of school lunch hot dogs would
explode simultaneously, spewing radioactive
gases into every school cafeteria in the free
world.

Chef Toxic hummed to himself as he used a
pastry decorator to draw some balloons on a

bacteria-infested birthday cake. Just as he reached for the rainbow jimmies, the door to the kitchen burst open with a crash. A small figure in a red cape and yellow costume with the letters MB on the chest stood in the door-way.

"Mmmffy Bfff!" Miss Flufferbrain cried.

The boy leaped into the room. "Lunchtime is over, tubby."

Aiming his gaze, Mighty Boy's powerful ultrared laser vision smashed a gigantic kitchen timer to pieces. Then Mighty Boy rushed over to the chemical vats, took a deep breath, and blew hard. The vats were covered instantly in a thick layer of ice. Satisfied that the chemicals were contained, Mighty Boy picked up the bacterial birthday cake and hurled it, his incredible strength causing it to crash through the wall.

"Oh, too bad, Toxic. You forgot to make a wish."

Chef Toxic scowled and grabbed a spatula with a three-inch spike on the end and ran over to Miss Flufferbrain. He held the spike up to her slender neck.

"One more step, midget man," Chef Toxic said, breathing heavily, "and she's mince-meat."

As quick as a flash, Mighty Boy sent a cart full of cupcake pans rolling right at Chef Toxic's large rear end. Chef Toxic fell backward on top of the cart, his hat landing in a bowl of acid-laced Cheez Whiz.

"YEOWWWW!" the villain screamed, running out of the kitchen. "You Mighty Brat. I'll get you for this!"

Mighty Boy untied Miss Flufferbrain and took the stuffing out of her mouth. She threw her arms around him and—

⚡

"Psst! Howard! Howard! You're humming the tune to *Mighty Boy* out loud!"

Miss Flufferbrain was just about to tell him how he'd made the world safe again for school hot dogs when someone punched him in the back.

"Howard!" hissed Maggie McDoren, who sat behind him. "Mrs. Fowler is talking to you!"

"Hello?" Mrs. Fowler's voice was loud. "Earth to Howard Weinstein, calling Howard Weinstein. Is anybody there?"

The laughter shook Howard out of his daydream.

"Uh, uh . . . yes?" His face was burning. He knew all the kids in class were staring at him.

"I'm sorry to interrupt you, Howard, but you're in school—math class, specifically—and I was wondering if you could join us?" Mrs. Fowler took a deep breath. "Taking out your math book and turning to page one hundred forty-seven would be an excellent beginning."

Howard leaned over to get his math book from under his desk, but Eddie Gervinsky, the big fat kid who sat in front of him, jerked his arm so that Howard almost fell out of his seat. Eddie laughed loudly. Howard put his math book on his desk and took out a clean sheet of paper. Then he adjusted his glasses and imagined Revenge Scene number 423: Eddie Gervinsky gets lifted high in the air and twirled around and around until finally being dumped headfirst into a garbage truck.

Starring Mighty Boy, *not* Howard Weinstein.

Mrs. Fowler shook her head sadly. "I think we'll need to have a little talk after school, Howard. Maybe with your parents."

Oh great, Howard thought, just what my parents need—more worrying. He'd just *had* a little talk with his science teacher, Mr. Vellors, the day before yesterday, and last week his little talk had been with Miss Turnley, the music teacher.

The talk was always the same: "Howard's day-dreaming . . . his head's in the clouds . . . he's got an overactive imagination . . . " The problem was that by now he'd gotten the talk so often he just . . . couldn't pay attention to it.

"I tried to warn you, Howard," whispered Maggie behind him. "You can't hum the theme song in class."

"Thanks," Howard whispered back as he flipped open his math book. So far Maggie'd been the only nice person in his class. But she was always too busy with her girlfriends, two of whom were snickering at him, to ever play after school.

Howard forced himself to concentrate on the perimeter of a triangle. But that reminded him of the *Mighty Boy* episode where Dr. Deranged learned the secrets of the Egyptian mummies and was able to make puca-puca juice, the only substance in the universe that could rob Mighty Boy of his powers and turn him into a regular boy.

A regular boy. That's what Howard used to be in his old school in California. He'd had friends there, but that felt so long ago. Howard's dad was a geologist and when he was offered a chance to teach for a year at New York University, his parents decided it would be fun to live in a big city for a while. Howard had thought so, too, but not anymore.

From the moment he walked into his fourth-grade classroom three months ago, Howard felt like an alien who'd landed in unfriendly territory. All the kids seemed two heads taller and twenty pounds heavier than him; he even overheard his mom telling his teacher that he was "small for his age." Plus he already knew most of the work they were covering, because his class in California had been an advanced one. That didn't exactly make him Mr. Popular.

And then there was Eddie Gervinsky, the bully who sat in front of him, who loved to tease him in school and on his way home, calling him four eyes and country hick.

After school was Howard's worst time of day. When he'd see all the other kids pairing off to go play together, he'd remember how he used to go fishing or hiking with his friends and would feel lonelier than ever. One day after school his mom felt bad for him and told him that after he finished his homework he could watch television. That's when it all started. It was around four o'clock and Howard was turning the knob of the channel changer impatiently. He paused for a second on Channel Six.

Howard watched as shy, meek Michael Boyer went into the boy's bathroom at school and changed himself into "Mighty Boy." He then battled the evil shape-shifter, Jelloid, who had transformed himself into Michael Boyer's French teacher, Miss Froofroo, and was planning to spray a deadly nerve gas all over the school. All the kids cheered as Mighty Boy karate-kicked Miss Froofroo and dumped her into the police car waiting outside.

Howard was hooked. Even though he knew Mighty Boy wasn't *really* shy and meek, he felt they had a special bond. He knew that one day Mighty Boy would help him show *his* true self . . . and help him become mighty.

Howard thought about Mighty Boy twenty-four hours a day; he was the first thing Howard saw every morning (when he opened his eyes and saw his Mighty Poster on the ceiling) and the last thing he saw every night (his Mighty Litey). Howard had Mighty Boy pajamas and matching underwear, a Mighty Boy notebook and pencil case, and for his last birthday his Aunt Suzy had given him a Mighty Boy skateboard (which he stayed on for fifteen seconds before falling off and breaking his glasses).

Howard was an honorary member of the Mighty Boy Boys' Club and he cherished every item he received, even the coupons for Mighty Bites cereal. He'd seen every episode of *Mighty Boy* on television, and had even memorized some of Mighty Boy's best lines. (His favorite was when Mighty Boy handed over Jelloid/Froofroo to the police: "Just top him with mini marshmallows, guys.")

The bell rang. Three o'clock. Eddie turned around and pretended to blow his nose on Howard's notebook. "Running home to watch *Mighty Boy*, Howie? Mighty Boy would knock *you* over with his toenail. Look! Up in the sky! Is it a bird? Is it a plane? No! It's Mighty Wimp!"

Howard packed up his books and walked to Mrs. Fowler's desk. She motioned for him to sit down while she filed some papers. He gazed out the window at the groups of kids walking home together. Maggie and her four friends were laughing hard about something. He got a little lump in his throat.

But then he sat up straight and remembered: he didn't need friends to walk home with. He had his best friend waiting for him every day at four o'clock right in his living room.

He had Mighty Boy.

Howard was sitting at the kitchen table after school, watching his mother furiously beat a chicken breast with a little wooden hammer. She was taking a cooking class at a gourmet cooking school nearby. It was one of the things "they could never do at their old house." That just made Howard miss their old house more. There he hadn't had to eat things like tonight's dinner, *cassoulet de poulet*, which was a fancy name for chicken casserole.

"How was school today, honey?" His mom pushed her long brown hair out of her eyes with the back of her hand.

Howard shrugged his shoulders. "Okay." He'd heard his parents discussing his "friend problem" at night and didn't want to worry his mom.

"Did you do anything fun? What did you play at recess?"

"Kick ball." Howard had been the last one picked, as usual.

His mom picked up the chicken breast and began slapping it between her hands, back and forth. Howard felt bad for the poor thing. Then he imagined Eddie Gervinsky as the chicken breast and smiled.

His mother thought he was smiling because he'd had fun playing kick ball at school.

"How about playing kick ball outside with a friend? Isn't there someone you'd like to invite over?" she asked.

Howard shook his head. They went through this every day. And every day he gave the same response. "Just Mighty Boy, Mom."

His mother grabbed a pepper mill and began grinding it high above the chicken. "I know you love Mighty Boy, Howard, but—"

"I know, I know; 'he's just an imaginary character.'"

"That's right," replied his mother. "And remember that the boy who plays Mighty Boy has problems just like you and me."

Howard sighed. It was useless to argue with her. But his mother was wrong: Howard's problem—his *only* problem—was that *he* wasn't Mighty Boy. If he were Mighty Boy, problems like school and friends and Eddie Gervinsky and glasses would disappear instantly.

"Howard, could you hand me that bowl of mushrooms?" His mom motioned toward the counter. "We're having mushroom pâté for an appetizer."

Howard passed the bowl of mushrooms to his mom. He was about to tell her how terrible mushroom pâté sounded when he got a pang of remembering mushroom hunting with his dad on one of their many camping trips. Howard couldn't think of anything he loved more in the world than those camping trips: catching their fish dinner in the small lake and frying it over an open fire, making gooey chocolate s'mores, and sleeping under the stars. Howard's dad knew everything there was to know about the outdoors: which berries were safe to eat, the name of the creepy crawlie in his sleeping bag, how to find your way by the stars, how to identify the smell of a nearby animal. Learning from his dad made Howard feel strong. When he was out in the woods, being "small for his age" didn't matter.

That was another bond between him and Mighty Boy: nature was the source of Mighty Boy's powers. After a battle with a supervillain, Mighty Boy would go into his private Mighty Cave and communicate telepathically with the animals of the forest.

The closest thing to a forest in Brooklyn was a big, woodsy park down the block from the Weinsteins' apartment. Howard used to stop at the park on his way home from school and climb trees or look for insects. But one day a couple of months ago, Eddie and his friend Barry were there shooting baskets. They followed Howard around and teased him so much that he had to leave.

On his way out of the park, he smelled something sweet; Howard turned and discovered a big, flowering sassafras tree. Right near it was an old, dead tree with a small, hollow opening in the trunk. A steady swarm of bees was going back and forth from the yellowish flowers of the sassafras tree to the hollow opening of the dead tree. It was probably packed with honeycombs from the bees, Howard thought. He waited until the bees had swarmed back to the sassafras tree, and then carefully put his hand in the hole and pulled out a small, golden honeycomb. Later, when he thought about showing his dad the tree, he decided against it; Eddie might still be at the park.

Now Howard glanced up at the clock—it was almost time. He quickly poured himself a bowl of Mighty Bites and went into the living room. He lowered the blinds and moved his cat off the green armchair. Then he turned on the television, settled back into the big chair, put up his feet, and took a big spoonful of cereal. This was it—the most perfect moment of the day.

The familiar theme music started, but instead of the usual opening credits, with Michael Boyer and his adopted family, Ma and Pa Boyer and little sister Lizzy, Mighty Boy appeared on the screen. Howard leaned forward and adjusted his glasses.

"Hi, Mighty Club members!" Mighty Boy did the Mighty Strike Hand Signal, which was how all Mighty Boy Boys' Club members were supposed to greet each other.

"Today is the big day! Are you guys as excited as I am?" Mighty Boy chuckled. Howard, still chewing his cereal, chuckled too. "Even *my* mighty powers can't tell me the name of the lucky guy who's going to be in one of my shows."

Howard gasped. The contest! He'd forgotten that they were announcing the winner today! He'd been so excited when Mighty Boy had announced that whoever wrote the best essay on "What Mighty Power Is the Most Valuable and Why?" would make a cameo appearance on *Mighty Boy* in New York. The essay was a cinch for Howard: he wrote about Mighty Boy's telepathic communication with animals. "Because animals in the wild are among the first to know when something is wrong in the natural world," he wrote, "they can warn Mighty Boy and help him save the planet." He stuck another spoonful of Mighty Bites into his mouth and started chewing even faster, then pulled the green chair up close to the television screen. Maybe if he stared at the screen hard enough, Mighty Boy would feel their secret spiritual bond.

"I'll announce the winner at the end of today's

show," Mighty Boy said. "So be patient, Mighty Guys, because that lucky name might just be yours!"

For once Howard hardly paid attention to the show. (Anyway, he'd seen it before.) Finally, after five commercials, Mighty Boy came back on the screen. He was holding a small white envelope.

"Okay, Mighty Guys. The time is NOW!"

That's what Mighty Boy said whenever he was gearing up to chase a bad guy. Howard had never figured out exactly what it was supposed to mean, but it sounded cool. Mighty Boy opened the envelope and held out a small piece of paper.

"And the winning essay was written by . . . "

The camera went in for a close-up. Howard leaned forward, stuck a soggy spoonful of cereal into his mouth, and held his breath.

". . . *Howard Weinstein* of Brooklyn, New York."

Howard opened his mouth. No sound came out—just a stream of Mighty Bites.

"Howard Weinstein," Mighty Boy was saying, "you are one *lucky* guy!"

"AAAAAHHHHHH!"

Howard's mother ran into the room, a look of panic on her face. She grabbed Howard by the shoulders. "What is it?"

Howard could barely speak. "He . . . M-Mighty . . . B-B-boy—"

"Yes? Yes? Mighty Boy what?"

"Picked . . . ME!" Howard shouted. *"To be on his show! I get to meet him and be in a show!"*

His mother laughed. "You're kidding! Are you sure it was *your* name?"

Howard nodded.

"Oh, that's terrific!" She gave him a hug. "I'm so happy for you, honey! Let's go call your dad."

His mom walked out of the room. Howard was stunned. He couldn't believe it . . . yet he had known it would happen someday. Howard Weinstein and Mighty Boy.

His dream was finally coming true.

3

"And before we leave today," said Mrs. Fowler, smiling at Howard, "let's all congratulate Howard Weinstein. He was chosen to play a small role on the *Mighty Man* show. I guess all that daydreaming pays off, Howard."

"It's 'Mighty *Boy*,'" said Howard, feeling a familiar flush as everyone turned to look at him. He'd had to tell Mrs. Fowler about his appearance because he was going to miss a few days of school; now he wished she hadn't said anything. A few kids were giggling.

"Wait until Mighty Boy gets a load of Mighty Dwarf," sneered Eddie. "He'll do some Mighty Laughing!"

Eddie had just gotten an extra close buzz cut, which made his head look smaller and his stomach look fatter. Eddie was famous for his fat stomach. Sometimes at recess he would lift up his T-shirt and make it jiggle around. Once he even drew a picture of a lady who moved when he jiggled.

Howard sighed and looked out the window. He thought that after yesterday's momentous announcement, *somebody* would be impressed and say something nice to him. But nothing happened. No one said anything. No one except Mrs. Fowler—and Eddie.

Just what he needed.

"Hey, I know! They'll call you Fearless Four Eyes!" Eddie laughed. He'd had a blue Popsicle at lunch. Eddie had spent the rest of the afternoon sticking out his tongue and moving it around really fast.

"They'd call *you* Super Dummy," muttered Howard under his breath.

Eddie narrowed his eyes. "What did you say?"

"Nothing." It was the first time Howard had ever said—or even whispered—anything back at Eddie.

Eddie lowered his voice. "If you called me what I think you called me, you're gonna be sorry. Very sorry."

Howard shrugged his shoulders and looked away, pretending he didn't care. He had felt mightier a second ago, when he'd called Eddie "Super Dummy." Now, though, he wished he could take it back.

Mrs. Fowler was telling the class what math homework to do; they'd be having a test on the material at the end of the week. Then the bell rang and everyone filed out. Eddie turned around, stuck his big foot under the front of

Howard's desk, and tipped it up. All of Howard's books and papers fell onto the floor. Eddie gave Howard a satisfied smirk as he left the class-room.

Howard sighed, packed up his things, and walked out of school. He thought about asking Maggie McDoren if she wanted to come over. But she'd already started down the steps with her usual group of girlfriends. Up ahead, he saw some boys in his class walking together. He sighed again, wishing he'd been invited to play with them. Howard decided to go a different way home.

Crossing the street, he slipped into an alley between two brownstones. Normally Howard was a little afraid of taking the alleys home; they were dark, and usually no one was around. But he did feel braver today because tomorrow was . . . *the big day*.

"Psst!"

Howard stopped. What was that? He waited and listened, his heart beating fast. There was no one around. He continued walking, this time faster. Someone could be hiding in a doorway or behind a Dumpster, he thought. Then he realized that this was exactly like the alley where Mighty Boy first encountered the evil Queen Barbazon and her zombie dolls. Although

Barbazon looked like a beautiful doll with her mane of blond hair and bright blue eyes, in reality she was a vampire, sucking the lifeblood out of innocent victims with her poisonous vacuum kiss. Her victims then became part of her ever-growing zombie army, who needed to vacuum kiss more and more victims in order to sustain themselves.

Howard walked faster. He could make out the end of the alley; it wasn't too far. . . .

Michael Boyer was innocently walking home from the grocery store, carrying a carton of milk for his mother, when he heard a strange sound. He stopped. His sonar hearing was activated. Danger was lurking nearby. But from where? Up ahead was a dark doorway. Should he approach it? Suddenly, from behind, he was thrown to the ground with amazing force! He wheeled around and stared up in horror. It was the zombie-doll army!

Plunk! Something hit Howard in the back. He stopped and looked down. It was a small rock. He turned around. Then he heard a high, shrill laugh. *Barbazon!* he thought.

No, no, not Barbazon, Howard knew. Some-one worse.

Eddie and Barry stepped out of a doorway.

"Well, if it isn't the little punk. He called me Super Dummy, Bare; can you believe that?" Eddie asked.

Howard ignored him and kept going. He was dying to start running but he didn't. He was mad at himself for being so stupid. This was the worst day to go through the alleys. Eddie ran in front of him, blocked his way, and put his face up close to Howard's. Eddie's breath smelled like bologna. He stuck out his blue tongue. Howard jerked around him and continued on. But then Barry ran in front of him and blocked his way again. Howard ran around Barry, but then Eddie blocked his way.

"Hey, it's a new dance," said Barry.

"Yeah, it's called Block the Twerp," said Eddie.

Howard felt his heart pounding. He had to get out of here, but how? Then he thought, Mighty Boy was in a situation just like this once. What did he do? . . .

Mighty Boy was panting hard . . . the zombie dolls were coming straight for him. The leader opened her eyes wide. Mighty Boy closed his;

he knew that if he looked too long into those
pinwheel blue eyes he'd be . . . lost. What
should he do? They'd expect him to turn and
run so instead, he ducked and plowed right
through them. . . .

Howard saw a small space between Eddie and
Barry. He pretended to turn away but then zipped
between them before they knew it.

Howard reached the sidewalk and looked
around. Now where? If only he were as smart as
Mighty Boy. He thought hard. . . .

Holding his nose to guard against the sweet,
hypnotizing perfume, Mighty Boy reached the
sidewalk. He needed to hide. He glanced
around quickly, then made a running leap over
a construction barricade, and landed in
between two buildings. . . .

Howard made a running leap over a moldy
pizza box, spotted a stairwell on the side of a
brownstone, and headed down the steps.

Crouching down in the little enclosure,
Howard tried to catch his breath. He peeked up
and saw Eddie and Barry on the sidewalk above

him. Eddie motioned for Barry to go around the building; he went the other way. Then they met back in front, searching the sidewalk for Howard. Suddenly Eddie turned in Howard's direction. Howard shot back down, but it was too late.

"I see you, *Mighty Wimp!*" Eddie sang out.

Howard dashed up out of the stairwell and made it to the back of the brownstone. He crouched behind a delivery van. He could hear Eddie coming. Panting hard, Howard flattened himself against the side of the building. When Eddie and Barry ran right past him, he couldn't believe his good luck. Mighty Boy always seemed to have that kind of luck . . . for a while. . . .

Mighty Boy, crouched behind a Dumpster, waited until he thought he'd lost the zombie dolls. He stood up and looked around carefully. Yep, it all seemed clear. He breathed a sigh of relief. Suddenly a giant zombie doll bolted up from inside the Dumpster! "Kiss him! Kiss him!" it screamed. . . .

"There he is!"

Howard jumped as Barry shouted, almost next to him. He veered around the brownstone again and took off down the block. Eddie and Barry were on his heels. Howard's lungs felt as if they were on fire. Every muscle in his body ached, but he had to keep going, just a little bit longer. I can do it, Howard thought, just like Mighty Boy. . . .

Exhausted, Mighty Boy didn't know if he could go on. . . . He closed his eyes and summoned a vision of Ouka, the snowy-tipped owl who was his teacher and master. . . . Oh, wise Ouka, send me your power. . . .

As Howard ran he frantically looked around for a place to hide; it was his only hope. Mighty Boy, he thought, give me your strength. . . .

Renewed with Ouka's power, Mighty Boy reached Barbazon's impenetrable penthouse. The fifty-story building was like a fortress; the only way in was through the front door. . . .

Howard saw a woman entering the front door of an apartment building. He *had* to get there. He *would* get there, just like Mighty Boy. Turning sharply, he dashed up the steps. Catch the door before it closes! he thought. Hurry!

Howard caught the door handle, but it slipped

out of his hand. He lost his balance and fell backward, scraping his elbow against the concrete steps.

Eddie and Barry were waiting at the bottom. They stood over him, panting and smiling.

"Did you fall and hurt yourself, little Mighty Wimp?" Eddie mocked. He threw back his head and laughed. "Get his book bag, Bare."

Barry pulled Howard's book bag off his shoulder. Howard was too exhausted to put up a fight. He managed to say weakly, "Give that back to me, Eddie."

Eddie laughed as he opened it. He took out Howard's math book and tossed it into a large puddle. Then he opened Howard's notebook. "Wow, straight As." Eddie looked thoughtful for a minute. "What did you call me today? Super Dummy? Well, I'm going to take pity on you. Instead of pounding your puny little body, I'm going to let you help me in math."

Howard rubbed his elbow; it hurt a lot.

Eddie smiled. "All you have to do is steal the math test from Mrs. Fowler's desk. A goody two-shoes like you shouldn't have any problem doing that, right?"

Howard didn't answer. He felt as low as a worm. Lower.

"Hey, Bare! Look at this!" Eddie held up a five-dollar bill. It was Howard's allowance for two months; he was saving up for some new *Mighty Boy* comic books.

"Thanks, Howard," said Eddie, pocketing the money. He leaned over, putting his face two inches from Howard's. "You better get that test for me, twerp, or you'll get a lot more than a sore elbow." Then Eddie yanked Howard's glasses off. He put them on and said, "Hey! I'm a four-eyed genius!"

Barry was doubled over in hysterics. Howard reached to take his glasses back, but Eddie held them high in the air.

"If you want your glasses back, repeat after me, Howard: I'm going to get that math test, or Eddie's going to be really mad."

"I'm going to get that math test, or Eddie's going to be really mad."

Eddie snapped off one side of Howard's glasses.

"Whoops! How clumsy of me!" he exclaimed. "Let's get out of here, Bare."

They were a little way down the sidewalk when Eddie turned around. "Maybe you can get your friend Mighty Boy to help you with that test."

They laughed and walked away. Howard picked up his glasses. What was he going to tell his mom? That a bully was picking on him? That he couldn't defend himself?

He started to pick up his schoolwork, but a

breeze blew the sheets all over the sidewalk. As he ran around chasing papers, he felt hot tears begin to form.

He had never felt so miserable in his life.

Eddie was right: he *was* Mighty Wimp.

Howard was standing behind a group of important-looking people in front of UBC Studios, trying to blend into the background. They were all waiting for Mighty Boy to arrive.

He felt terrible on what should have been the best day of his life. He'd had to put masking tape on his glasses to hold them together. Howard knew that as soon as Mighty Boy saw him, he'd just think that Howard was a wimp. Only wimps wore glasses like that.

A tall man in a suit walked up to him. "I'll bet you're Howard Weinstein," he said. "I'm Mr. Levine, the producer of *Mighty Boy*."

"H-hello." Howard's voice sounded terrible—high and squeaky.

"Nervous?" Mr. Levine asked, smiling.

Howard nodded. He didn't want to squeak.

"Perfectly natural, buddy. Perfectly natural." Mr. Levine gave him a little punch in the arm.

Howard tried to smile. When he'd finally gotten home yesterday, he'd told his parents that he'd scored the tie-breaking goal in a kick ball game but then tripped, breaking his glasses. When his mother said that she'd been ready to call the police, he suddenly got mad. Howard told her that he was sick of being treated like a baby and that he was just late and that she was making a big deal out of nothing. Then he stomped upstairs and wouldn't even come down to watch the end of *Mighty Boy*. (He knew it was a rerun.)

Howard hadn't mentioned having to steal the math test. But it was hard for him to put it out of his mind, even while standing here waiting for Mighty Boy.

Then Howard saw a big black car turn down the block, and he forgot all about the math test. It was *his* car, Howard knew, feeling a shiver of excitement. The black car stopped right in front of the studio, and the chauffeur hopped out and opened the back door. Howard held his breath. He couldn't believe that Mighty Boy was going to be coming out of that car door.

Howard watched as a shoe emerged from the car, then a leg, then a chest, then—Howard need-ed to exhale—*Him*! It was Mighty Boy! Howard thought he might faint; his legs felt wobbly. Sud-denly Mr. Levine came over, put his arm around Howard, and propelled him through the crowd.

"Mighty Boy," said Mr. Levine, pushing Howard forward, "this is Howard Weinstein."

Mighty Boy turned around. Howard gazed up at him, feeling his stomach somersault. Mighty Boy looked enormous in person: taller and older than twelve, which Howard knew was his real age.

His light-blond hair, gently windblown, shimmered in the sunlight; his eyes were so blue they looked like jewels. Howard just stared at him, his mouth slightly open. Mighty Boy held up his hand in the Mighty Strike Hand Signal position. Howard blinked, then realized what he was supposed to do. He managed to make a small fist and lightly touch the palm of Mighty Boy's hand.

Mighty Boy snorted. "What was that? I could hardly feel it!"

Everyone laughed. Howard felt his familiar flush.

"How about trying it again, Howie?" asked Mr. Levine, looking at Mighty Boy.

Mighty Boy sighed and lifted his hand. Howard made a fist and hit it hard. Everyone cheered.

"That's more like it, Howie," said Mr. Levine. "Okay if we call you Howie?"

Howard nodded even though he'd never liked the nickname.

Mr. Levine motioned for everyone to follow him into the studio. Howard glided along behind Mighty Boy, taking two steps for his every one. Howard felt he was in a dream.

"So how old are you again, Howie? About seven?" asked Mr. Levine.

"Nine," said Howard, relieved that his voice didn't squeak. "I'm in fourth grade. I'm . . . small for my age."

"Yeah, you sure are—" Mighty Boy began, but Mr. Levine nudged him in the ribs. He cleared his throat. "I mean . . . uh, well, you'll probably catch up . . . soon."

Howard felt his face get hot again.

They'd reached a large open space with cameras and spotlights. People with headphones were talking to each other, moving equipment around. Howard got excited; this must be the place where they were going to film the show. Then he saw Mighty Boy's "mother," Ma Boyer.

"Hey," he shouted, pointing at the lady, "there's your mother!"

Mighty Boy burst out laughing. So did everyone else. Mr. Levine said, "That's not his real mother, Howie. That's the actress who plays her on TV."

Howard felt like a dummy. "I knew that," he said under his breath.

Mighty Boy chatted with a few of the cameramen. Howard watched as they laughed and joked around together. Mighty Boy looked so comfortable here. Everything about him was perfect, absolutely perfect. Howard felt smaller than ever. What kind of special bond was he thinking about earlier? That they'd be best friends? It was almost funny, except that Howard didn't feel like laughing.

Carrying a clipboard, Mr. Levine walked over to Howard.

"Okay, the plan today is for you guys to have some lunch together, get to know each other, then you can watch us film a bit of the show and see how it's done." He smiled. "Today we just want you to relax, meet some of the crew, walk around the sets, whatever you want to do. On Friday we'll rehearse a bit, then do the scene. Sound okay?"

Howard nodded. Lunch with Mighty Boy. They were going to eat *together*.

A guy with a Mighty Boy T-shirt brought in two big bags.

"Great! Chow!" shouted Mighty Boy. "I'm so hungry I could eat a sponsor!"

Everyone laughed. So did Howard, although he didn't get the joke. Mighty Boy motioned for him to sit down in one of the canvas director's chairs. Then he opened his bag of food.

"Great," he said, stuffing a french fry into his mouth. "Jumbo-burgers and a chocolate shake. My favorite meal."

"Mine too," said Howard quickly, although he'd never had a Jumbo-burger in his life.

Howard opened his bag and took out his hamburger; it seemed the size of a football. There was no way he'd be able to eat it all. Mighty Boy, he noticed, had already eaten half of his. Howard ate about a quarter of his burger, a few fries, and took three sips of his chocolate shake. He thought he would burst.

Mighty Boy gulped his milkshake. "You're never gonna get bigger if you don't eat more, you know."

"I know," Howard said softly. He took a small bite out of his burger.

"Mind if I finish your shake?"

Mind? Howard shook his head and handed him the cup. He'd have to keep it as a souvenir. It had Mighty Boy's germs.

Mighty Boy finished his food and stretched back in his chair. "So is there anything in particular you want to see?"

"Yeah," Howard answered excitedly. He'd been hoping for this. "I'd love to see the Mighty Mobile. Maybe I could get a ride in it."

Mighty Boy laughed. "I don't think so. The Mighty Mobile doesn't really exist; it's just some props and a backdrop. So is most of the stuff on the show."

Howard nodded; he didn't know what props and a backdrop were, and he didn't care. He was in heaven, sitting in a director's chair next to Mighty Boy. His knee was *almost* touching Mighty Boy's knee. He leaned back and took a deep breath. This *was* the greatest day of his life, even if he did have to wear glasses with tape on the side.

He gave himself a little pinch on the arm just to make sure that he wasn't daydreaming.

He smiled.

The pinch hurt.

5

"Honey, could you open this jar of pickles for me?"

"Sure, Mom," replied Mighty Boy. He gave a yank, and the pickles fell all over the floor. "Whoops!" He smiled sheepishly. Howard, watching from the side, smiled sheepishly too.

Ma Boyer put her hands on her hips, tapped her foot, and gave her son a stern look.

Mighty Boy shrugged. "Sorry, Mom. I guess I just don't know my own strength. How about if I reheat your coffee?"

Before she could answer, Mighty Boy stared at the cup on the counter. Howard waited to see the red beam, but all he heard was the little buzzing sound that meant Mighty Boy was using his laser vision. Ma Boyer ran over to the counter.

"No! Stop!"

She picked up the cup and, holding it over the sink, poured out a thick white liquid. "That was your sister's ice cream!"

Mighty Boy giggled and put his hand over his mouth. "Whoops again! Sorry, Mom!"

He put up his palms and shrugged, looking at the camera. Howard laughed; this was one of his favorite parts of the show—when Mighty Boy did something too mighty at home and his mom got a little mad at him.

"Cut! That's a take!" someone yelled. "Great job, MB."

Howard was thrilled. They were calling Mighty Boy "MB" on the set. That was so cool. Now Howard was like . . . part of the crew.

When he was sure the scene was finished, Howard walked over to Mighty Boy, who was wiping his face with a towel. "That was so funny! When you melted the ice cream by mistake!"

Mighty Boy gave him a tight smile. "Thanks."

"But I didn't see your laser vision," said Howard.

Mighty Boy sighed. "That's a special effect. They put that in after we do the scene."

A burly man in a sweat suit approached them. "So, MB, did you practice? Or am I going to have to go easy on you like I always do?"

"Just wait and see," said Mighty Boy, smiling.

The man extended his hand to Howard. "Hi, I'm Ron. MB's karate coach."

Howard shook his hand.

"Maybe MB could show you some of his karate tricks," Ron said. "We usually have our lesson next door."

Mighty Boy grabbed Ron's arm and tried to throw him over his shoulder, horsing around. Howard watched them for a while, feeling awkward; he wasn't sure what to do. Then he remembered that Mr. Levine had told him to look around the studio if he wanted to. There were two sets in this studio, Mr. Levine had explained to him: the Mighty Boy kitchen and another one that doubled as the Mighty Cave or a supervillain's hideout. The show also did a lot of filming outdoors, Mr. Levine said. In fact, Howard's scene was to take place in Wintergreen Forest, a state park about twenty miles outside New York City. So on top of meeting Mighty Boy and being on his show, Howard was going to a real forest. He hadn't been in a real forest since he'd left California.

A lady pushing a rack stuffed with clothes almost ran into Howard. As she passed by, he could see Mighty Boy's costume hanging in front. He gasped softly: there it was! He couldn't *wait* to see Mighty Boy in his costume.

Howard walked around until he reached a set of stairs at the far end of the studio. He wouldn't mind finding a bathroom; he hadn't seen one anywhere. He went down the stairs. At the bottom, he opened a heavy door and peered down a dark hallway. There were some doors, but he couldn't tell what they were in the dark; one of them was probably a bathroom. He took a few steps inside. The door closed behind him with a *slam*! It made him jump.

The hallway was almost pitch-black. There

didn't seem to be anyone around. Howard decided he didn't need a bathroom that badly after all and turned around to leave. But the door wouldn't open. Howard twisted the knob, throwing all his weight against it, but the door wouldn't budge.

It was locked.

He was locked in the hallway.

The *dark* hallway.

He took a deep breath and told himself not to be scared. Of course there was a way out. He just had to get there.

"H-hello? Anybody here?"

No answer. Not a sound. He took some small steps, staying right next to the wall, feeling it as he went along. The hallway seemed tremendously long.

Finally he reached an end. But it really wasn't an end; the hallway just turned. He continued down another dark hallway which then turned, and down another. It was like he was in a maze. Why wasn't there a light anywhere? And no noise? Why couldn't he hear anything from the studio above? It suddenly seemed impossible that there *was* a studio upstairs. What if no one discovered that he was missing? What if he'd found an underground place that no one knew existed and . . . there was something else down here. . . .

Howard's heart felt like it was going to pound out of his chest.

He had to get out of here.

He started to run, going around one corner, then another. There had to be an end. He *had* to come to the end.

Finally he came to a door. Holding his breath, he twisted the knob. The door opened. Howard felt almost weak with relief. Stepping inside, he found himself in a large, dimly lit room that looked like a kitchen. Not like his kitchen at home, though; more like one you'd find in a restaurant. Silver-colored pots and pans hung low from the ceiling. In a corner two large white kettles sat on top of a gigantic stove. Against another wall stood a floor-to-ceiling steel refrigerator and freezer. The freezer had a massive steel handle that was almost the size of Howard's entire body. Howard felt his sense of relief going away. Fast.

That handle.

He *knew* that handle.

In fact, he *knew* this entire kitchen.

But from where?

Then he noticed something white hanging from a hook in the corner. He couldn't make out what it was. Howard took a few steps closer and gasped. It was a large white chef's hat.

Chef Toxic!

This was Chef Toxic's kitchen!

He ran back to the door he'd come through. Locked. Frantically, he looked for a way out. He ran to another door next to the refrigerator and opened it, trying to remember what it led to. It was pitch-black inside. He felt around on the wall for a light switch; he found one and flipped it on.

Howard's eyes widened. On the shelves of this small room were boxes and containers. *Sulfuric Acid* was written on one, *Potassium Paste* on another. There was *Mutagen Mix* and *Toxic Tonic*. It was Chef Toxic's storage closet! Of course! How could Howard have forgotten!

Howard closed his eyes and tried hard to remember the maze of underground tunnels that led to Chef Toxic's kitchen. That's where he must have been before. Then he remembered that there was a way out of the kitchen around the side of the stove. He ran over and found himself in another hallway. At the end of it was a T—he could go either way.

Directly in front of him was another door. He wasn't sure what to do. He tried the knob. It turned. Should he go inside?

Suddenly he heard a noise. It came from the direction of the kitchen. It was a slow, creaking noise, like someone walking who . . . didn't want to be discovered. Howard's pulse began to race. Oh no, someone was after him! *Chef Toxic!*

Howard opened the door and hurled himself through. It was dark, and he couldn't find a switch. The creaking stopped but then Howard heard very soft footsteps. Someone was sneaking up on him. The steps got closer. He tried to scream, but his voice was gone.

Howard was frozen in terror.

It became quiet. He put his ear to the door. Whoever was out there knew that Howard was inside. Oh, no. What should he do now?

He had to make a run for it.

Taking a deep breath, Howard grabbed the doorknob, flung open the door, and ran— *smack!*—right into someone. Someone big and fat in white clothes with a buzz cut. Eddie Gervinsky! *No, worse . . . Chef Toxic!*

Howard screamed.

A man tried to grab him. Howard ran through the kitchen. The door was open now. He ran as fast as he could down the dark hallway.

"Help! Help! He's after me!"

He could hear the man running after him. It was just a matter of seconds before the man would catch him. Howard turned the corner and crashed into someone else. The person took hold of Howard's shoulders and wouldn't let him go.

Oh, no! Who now? Jelloid? Barbazon?

Howard closed his eyes. He felt like he might pass out.

"Howard! Howard!"

He opened his eyes.

Mr. Levine was holding him. Next to him were

Mighty Boy and the lady who played Mighty Boy's mother. They were all staring at him.

"It's Chef Gervin—I mean, Chef Toxic—he's, he's . . . " Howard could barely speak, he was panting so hard.

Mighty Boy stepped forward and put his hand on Howard's shoulder. "Howard, calm down, everything's okay."

"Take deep breaths," said the lady who played the mother.

The fat man came jogging around the corner. Now Howard could see that it wasn't anyone he knew; it wasn't even Chef Toxic. It was some guy in a white sweatshirt that said *UBC Studio Staff*.

"Are you okay?" he asked. Howard nodded.

The man took a deep breath. "Whew! You almost scared the pants off me." He turned to the others. "I was going to get some props out of closet two-B when the door burst open and he ran into me!"

Everyone started to laugh.

Everyone except Howard.

6

Howard had made up his mind even *before* he walked into class, tripped over Eddie's foot, and almost went flying across the floor.

After what happened at UBC Studios, Howard decided that enough was enough: he was going to steal the math test.

Sure, he knew stealing was bad, but he wanted to solve his own problems, just like Mighty Boy did. He didn't want to run home and tell his parents that Eddie Gervinsky was bullying him. So he came up with a great plan: he'd steal the math test, *show* it to Eddie, and then tell Mrs. Fowler. She might get a little mad about it, but at least everyone would know that Howard Weinstein *could* steal a math test if he wanted to.

That would show Eddie.

After school Howard slipped into the boys' bathroom to figure out a plan (and also to avoid Eddie on the way home). He stood tottering on top of the toilet seat in the last stall, waiting until school cleared out.

When it became quiet in the hall, Howard slipped out. He caught a glimpse of himself in the mirror. The tape on his glasses—colored with brown Magic Marker—looked stupider than ever. Suddenly he couldn't stand how dumb he looked, and he yanked his glasses off. He glared at himself in the mirror, refusing to squint.

He filled his hands with water from the sink and smoothed back his hair. Yeah, he looked a lot cooler this way, no doubt about it. Now he didn't look at all like Mighty Wimp. In fact, he looked a little like Proto-Punk, the bratty supervillain who challenged Mighty Boy to baby-ish, but dangerous, games like musical exploding chairs and pin the tail on the mutant. Proto-Punk once kidnapped Mighty Boy's little next-door neighbor, Billy, to force Mighty Boy to go on a scavenger hunt. Besides having to find a peanut, a piece of bubble gum, and a shoelace, Mighty Boy had to find the nuclear detonator that Proto-Punk had hidden somewhere. With just seconds to spare, Mighty Boy figured out that it was stuck on Mr. Potato Head's nose, an ingenious spot.

Howard sneered at himself in the mirror the way Proto-Punk sneered at Mighty Boy. Yeah, he thought, I could act the same way, if I felt like it. I'm ready to steal that math test. And, putting his glasses back on, Howard went to the door, stuck his head out, and checked both ways down the hall. Mrs. Fowler's room was dark. No one was coming—the coast was clear.

Howard zipped into the classroom. So far so good.

Mrs. Fowler's desk was perfectly clean except for her monthly class schedule. Howard had no idea if she kept the tests in the desk or somewhere else. He opened the top desk drawer, and found some homework sheets, pencils, paper clips, and a bag of potato chips. Howard was tempted to take the chips; he was hungry. But he decided against it—Proto-Punk would find the test before anything else. He opened another drawer: some math books, more homework sheets, and a bottle of antacid. No tests in the desk.

He looked at the clock. It was three forty-five. He'd told his mother he was staying after school to do a science project with some kids from his class.

Looking around the room, Howard tried to think where else Mrs. Fowler might keep test papers. The tall file cabinet in the corner! Howard quickly dragged over a chair and opened the top drawer of the cabinet. Right in front of his face was a file labeled Division and Multiplication Tests. Howard almost fell off his chair. This was it! He took out the file.

As he hopped down from the chair, he heard a noise outside in the hall. He ran over to the door, turned out the lights, and flattened himself against the wall. Without thinking, Howard had left the door partly open. All he could see was a wide gray mop. It was Murray, the after-school janitor. Was he going to come into Mrs. Fowler's room? Howard started to get nervous.

Then he remembered Proto-Punk. Proto-Punk would tell Murray to get lost, vamoose, make like a tree and leave. Howard put on his best Proto-Punk sneer and held his breath, waiting for Murray. But the janitor just moved on down the hall, humming a song to himself. After a few seconds Howard poked his head out the door. Murray was turning at the end of the hallway. *Yeah!* Proto-Punk Howard was on a roll.

Howard carried the chair back to the desk and put the test on top of his book bag. He was ready to leave. Then it suddenly occurred to him that stealing this test was turning out to be a cinch, as easy as pie. Hey, what's the big hurry? Howard thought. Proto-Punk would take his time, snoop through some more files, make himself comfortable.

Howard stretched and remembered the bag of potato chips in Mrs. Fowler's desk. "She won't miss it," he said to himself. He got the chips out of the drawer, sat down, put his feet up on the desk in front of him. He opened the bag and started munching. Just like Proto-Punk. Yessiree. Just how many "wimps" would—or could—steal a division test so easily? Not many, he'd bet. Because people who steal tests aren't wimps—they're daredevils, ready to take risks, willing to stare in the face of danger and laugh.

Howard threw his head back and laughed. He choked on a potato chip. Then the lights went on.

"Maybe you'd like to tell me what's so funny?"

Mrs. Fowler was standing in the doorway.

Howard tried to jump up, but his legs were on the desk in front of him, so he tipped backward—and fell off the chair.

"Miss-Miss-Missus Fowler," he stammered, still choking on a chip. "What are you . . . I mean, what am I . . . I mean, I . . . I came back to . . . to . . . get m-my . . . homework."

Mrs. Fowler snorted and walked over to him. "And what is your homework doing in the file cabinet?"

"Uh, uh . . ." Howard looked up; he hadn't closed the drawer. He let out a low moan. What an idiot! A minute ago, he had been Proto-Punk, breezing along, laughing in the face of danger, and the next minute . . . he was dead meat. "I . . . I . . . thought, uh, maybe you, uh, filed it?"

"Nice try, Howard. But you'll have to think faster than that if you're going to be a cheater." She picked up the test on top of Howard's book bag. "Hmm. Division test. You don't need the division test; you're good at division."

Mrs. Fowler tapped her foot, waiting for an

explanation. He couldn't tell her that because of Eddie he was stealing the test to prove that he wasn't Mighty Wimp and that he wasn't going to use it to cheat, but just to show. It all seemed so complicated suddenly. So he didn't say anything.

"And"—Mrs. Fowler's voice rose—"is that *my* bag of potato chips?"

Howard nodded miserably.

"Isn't that a little low?"

Howard nodded miserably again.

"Are you stealing this test for someone else? Someone with the initials *E.G.*, perhaps?"

Howard shook his head.

Mrs. Fowler leaned back against the desk. "Come on, Howard. I know this isn't for you. Why don't you tell me what it's all about?"

"It's about me looking for the test, that's all," Howard said, rubbing his greasy hands on his pants. "I forgot my division."

Mrs. Fowler sighed. "You're making this difficult, Howard. I'm going to have to tell the principal. We'll call your parents."

He narrowed his eyes at her. So? Big wow. Proto-Punk wouldn't care who she called. Call the marines, Howard thought.

"Is something wrong with your eyes, Howard?" Mrs. Fowler asked.

He unnarrowed his eyes, shrugged his shoulders, and tried to look dumb, like Eddie. It wasn't too hard.

"They'll probably pull you off the *Mighty Boy* show."

Oh, no. Howard hadn't thought of that. Would his parents do that? He had no idea; he'd never done anything like this before.

"I could even recommend it to them," Mrs. Fowler warned.

Howard sighed deeply. Proto-Punk was gone. Long gone. He'd made like a tree and left.

"Yeah," he said softly. "It was for Eddie."

"I knew it," replied Mrs. Fowler.

"But now he's going to beat me up," Howard said, suddenly on the verge of tears. It wasn't the thought of Eddie beating him up that did it—it was . . . everything else.

Mrs. Fowler came over and put her arm around his shoulders. "No, he's not. We're going to talk to the principal and have him dealt with. Maybe we'll suspend him for a few days or transfer him to a different class, but we'll make sure he leaves you alone."

Howard knew that it wouldn't make any difference. Eddie would find a way to get to him.

Howard wished the earth would open and swallow him up. Then he wouldn't be able to make things worse for himself.

The cast and crew were already piling into a bus for the ride out of town when Howard arrived at the studio that morning. He still felt a little embarrassed about what had happened the other day, but when he saw that there was an empty seat next to Mighty Boy, he forgot all about it. As they drove out of the city, Howard was getting ready to tell Mighty Boy about his problem with Eddie and ask for some advice. But then Mr. Levine, who was sitting in front of them, turned around and started talking to Mighty Boy about the Yankees. Howard didn't know much about the Yankees—he only followed the small baseball team in his town in California—so he just looked out the window.

Mrs. Fowler had driven Howard home from school after finding him with the test. She had promised him that Eddie would be taken care of and that Howard had nothing to worry about. That was easy for her to say, he'd thought to himself. After he was dropped off, he could have sworn he'd seen Eddie standing in the doorway of the little grocery store across the street. But when he looked again, Eddie was gone. Howard quickly ran into his building. His mother, with her usual antennae, had guessed that something was wrong, but Howard said he was just tired. He went to bed early but had a hard time falling asleep.

Now he felt better. Gazing out the bus window, Howard saw a sign for Wintergreen Forest. The bus turned right and went some distance down a dirt road. Howard couldn't believe it: suddenly they were in a dark, dense woods with all kinds of trees—oak and maple, pine and birch—just like the woods near his house in California.

"All out!"

Stepping off the bus, Howard took a deep breath and smiled; it smelled like home.

Mr. Levine came over to him. "Howard, are you okay with your lines?"

Howard nodded. His lines were "No, I didn't see anything" and "Good luck, Mighty Boy."

Howard was to play a boy who's hiking in the woods. Mighty Boy comes upon him while he's searching for the evil Rainiac, a supervillain who makes vaporous clouds filled with bacterial "rain." Rainiac has situated a cloud over Mighty Boy's mother, Ma Boyer, who is planting zucchini in the backyard. The rain will begin in one hundred seconds if Mighty Boy does not reveal the source of his secret powers to Rainiac. But Mighty Boy can't do that, of course, and must track down Rainiac in his cave laboratory before it's . . . TOO LATE.

Mr. Levine sent Howard to the makeup trailer

to get ready. There, a lady with dyed red hair led him to a chair in front of a big mirror with lots of lights around it. She rubbed some goop on his face, put lipstick on him (which she said would look "perfectly natural" in front of the camera), and sprayed stinky stuff on his hair. She asked him if he absolutely needed to wear his glasses. He nodded unhappily. At least he now had new glasses, so he wouldn't have to wear masking-taped ones on national television.

Next, he went to wardrobe for a pair of hiking shorts and a T-shirt. They also gave him a backpack stuffed with paper to make it look full. Howard tried to tell the lady that no one would go hiking in a forest like this one with shorts on; you'd get all bitten up. But she simply gave him a blank look and told him that she had her orders from the director.

Howard stepped out of the trailer. They were filming a scene nearby: Mighty Boy was holding up his hands and rubbing his fingers to detect signs of bacterial rain. Behind him on a tall branch sat Ouka, the wise owl. Howard gazed at the bird: it looked a lot smaller, and its feathers weren't as snowy white as they appeared on television. But Mighty Boy looked fabulous in his red-and-yellow costume. The shiny material showed off Mighty Boy's powerful arm and stomach muscles. Howard would give anything to have stomach muscles.

"Yes, I can detect minute signs of bacterial vapors in the air, Ouka. Rainiac must have passed through here," Mighty Boy was saying. His voice sounded older, more grown-up than when he was just talking.

Howard hadn't seen them bringing Ouka; the person who took care of him must have come by car.

"We must warn the other creatures, Ouka. A drop of Rainiac's rain will destroy this entire forest and everything in it. They will all die." Mighty Boy's voice had dropped to a whisper. He looked as if he might cry. Howard felt like he might cry too. Mighty Boy was such a great actor.

"Cut! Perfect! Great scene, MB!" the director shouted enthusiastically.

Howard walked up to Mighty Boy. "Who takes care of Ouka?"

Mighty Boy laughed. "No one. This Ouka is stuffed. We only use a real one at the studio in New York."

"Oh," said Howard. He felt sort of foolish. No wonder it looked so small. Now that he looked closer, he could see the bird was fake.

The director raised his voice. "Attention, everyone! The next scene calls for Howard Weinstein. Who's Howard?"

Mr. Levine came over to Howard and put his hand on his shoulder. "Here he is. Our guest of honor."

Howard blushed a little as the director gripped his hand and shook it hard. "Hi, Howard; I'm Adam. Nice to meet you. Your scene is up now. Get ready."

"Okay," said Howard. "I . . . think I'm ready."

"You have to *know* you're ready." Adam smiled.

Howard smiled back but felt a little uneasy. Adam seemed nice but was very busy and businesslike.

"Okay, people!" Adam shouted. "Is everyone ready?"

Howard put on his backpack, and an assistant director showed him what to do. He was supposed to walk slowly, as if he were simply enjoying a walk in the woods. He felt a little nervous. Everyone here knew what to do except him.

"Remember, Howard, Mighty Boy says his line first," reminded Adam. "Then you say yours."

"Right," said Howard, going over his lines in his head for the umpteenth time.

"Okay? Lights! Camera! Action!" Adam pointed to Howard.

Howard walked slowly and smiled to show how much he was enjoying himself.

"Cut! Howard, don't smile so much. You look

sort of strange. Just a pleasant look on your face is fine."

Howard nodded. He'd do it right now.

"Okay, everyone. Action!"

Howard walked slowly and didn't smile as much. He heard Mighty Boy behind him.

"Greetings, hiker!"

Howard cleared his throat. "No, I didn't see anything."

"Cut! Howard, you have to wait until Mighty Boy asks you if you saw anything."

Howard waved and nodded. He'd do it right this time.

They started again. "Greetings, hiker!" called Mighty Boy.

Howard waited.

"Have you seen a suspicious-looking man coming through here?" asked Mighty Boy.

Howard shook his head. "Yeah—I mean, no— I did, uh . . . "

"Cut!"

Mighty Boy rolled his eyes and muttered something about what they had to put up with for the sponsors. Adam nodded and motioned to Mighty Boy to talk to Howard. Sighing, Mighty Boy walked over.

"Let me give you some tips, Howard," Mighty Boy said. "First of all, relax. Don't keep saying the lines over and over to yourself. Try to forget about the cameras. Okay?"

Howard nodded, trying to ignore the queasy feeling in his stomach.

"Okay, everyone," Adam called out. "Take four!"

"Greetings, hiker!" said Mighty Boy. "Have you seen a suspicious-looking man coming through here?"

"No, I haven't seen anything," Howard replied.

Mighty Boy nodded. "Be careful in these woods."

Howard nodded back. "Good duck, Mighty Boy."

They did twelve more "takes." Howard still didn't get it right. On the thirteenth take, Howard said "Good puck, Flighty Toy," and almost started crying. Adam (who almost started crying too) had to go into the makeup trailer and count to ten. Howard felt like a complete and total idiot.

Mr. Levine strode onto the set. "Okay, everyone, break time! Let's take a breather."

Howard sighed. Mighty Boy came over to him.

"I don't think I can do it," said Howard softly, looking down.

"Yes, you can, Howie," Mighty Boy assured him. "It's just the first-time jitters."

Mr. Levine approached them. "I have an idea. Why don't you guys take a little walk in the woods to relax?"

Mighty Boy shook his head. Mr. Levine gave him a look.

"Okay, okay." Mighty Boy shrugged.

Mr. Levine consulted a clipboard. "Derek and Bob are getting lunch, then scouting locations around a suspension bridge. It says here that to reach it on foot, you just follow the blue markers on the trees." He smiled at Howard. "It'll take your mind off your lines."

"Okay," Howard replied, feeling that he would never, ever, ever get those lines right.

He wished he were anywhere but here.

"The first time is always tough," Mighty Boy said as they turned onto the forest path. "Until you get used to it."

"So it was hard for you too?" Howard felt better knowing that Mighty Boy had also flubbed his lines the first time in front of the camera.

"Well, not for me, but everyone else says that," replied Mighty Boy. "I've grown up in front of the camera, so I'm pretty relaxed. I was one and a half the first time I was on television, in a baby food commercial." He snickered. "When I got older I made my parents get all the copies of it and burn them."

Howard laughed.

"I mean, sure, everyone says that I'm a natural, supertalented, and all that." Mighty Boy swatted at some flies buzzing near his head. "But I still have to rehearse like everybody else."

Howard stopped to pick up a piece of bark. He saw his shadow just slightly behind him, which meant it was around 11:00 A.M. His dad had drummed into him so many times that you should always keep track of where the sun is by your shadow in the woods that he just automatically noticed it. "But you *are* supertalented. You're a great actor. I remember when you had to fight Jelloid, after he'd transformed himself into your mother. And you had to keep remembering that it was Jelloid you were fighting, but it was really hard. You were so torn up about it, I . . . I . . ." Howard couldn't finish.

"I know. That was one of my best scenes ever. One of the sponsors said she started crying," Mighty Boy remarked.

"And what about learning the lines?" asked Howard. "I think it's so hard to memorize."

"Well, I have a photographic memory, so I only have to see something once and I instantly remember it," said Mighty Boy.

"I wish I had that," said Howard. "I'm never going to get those lines right."

Mighty Boy shrugged. "Not if you think that way, you won't."

Howard thought for a minute. This was the perfect time. "I've been wanting to talk about a problem I have. There's this kid in my class, Eddie Gervinsky. He calls me four eyes and he pushes me around and now he wants me to steal a—"

"Listen!" said Mighty Boy, interrupting him. "What's that noise? An airplane?"

Howard stopped and listened. "No, it's rushing water. Probably a waterfall."

"Really?" remarked Mighty Boy. "Let's try to find it."

He ran ahead; Howard followed him. Mighty Boy wasn't even listening to him. And why should he? Howard thought. Mighty Boy doesn't need anyone to solve *his* problems for him.

Howard caught up with Mighty Boy, who was standing on top of a large rock. Howard climbed up next to him and looked around. "I don't see a waterfall. It must be farther away than it sounds. And we should make sure we see some blue markers—"

"Over there!" exclaimed Mighty Boy, running off.

Howard wasn't sure the waterfall was in the direction that Mighty Boy was pointing to, but he didn't want to say anything.

"Wait," called Howard.

Mighty Boy was going up a small slope, his red cape flashing between the trees. Howard, who was several paces behind him, heard a pecking sound and looked up. A red-bellied woodpecker sat high in the tree next to him. Howard got excited: his dad was an amateur bird-watcher, and Howard knew almost all the kinds of birds around their old house in California. But this one, Howard knew, lived only in the East; he couldn't wait to tell his dad.

After a few minutes of watching the woodpecker, Howard jogged to catch up to Mighty Boy. The sun was directly overhead now; Howard could barely see his shadow. It must be around noon, he thought, feeling a bit hungry.

Up a little way, Mighty Boy had stopped.

Howard came up behind him.

"Listen. Can you hear it now?" asked Mighty Boy.

Howard strained to listen. He heard something. "Yeah. I think I do hear it."

"It's over here." Mighty Boy pointed to his left. "I know it. Come on. Let's race!"

They dashed off together. Suddenly the world seemed magical and nothing could be wrong: Howard was running through a beautiful forest with Mighty Boy. The roar of rushing water got louder, and when they finally caught a glimpse of the waterfall, they both yelped.

"Wow!" exclaimed Mighty Boy when they reached the waterfall. "I can't believe it! I've never seen anything like this before. It's huge!"

Howard nodded. The waterfall was at least twenty feet high, and its roar was deafening. They sat down on a big rock and watched it, feeling the cool spray against their faces.

After a while they climbed on top of some rocks and found small stones to throw into the water. Howard dropped some leaves and branches down, and they watched them move through the current.

Howard turned away from the waterfall. His stomach was growling again. He looked for his shadow. It was a little in front of him; it was probably around twelve-thirty now. They were supposed to have lunch when they reached Bob and Derek near the suspension bridge.

"Are you hungry?" Howard asked.

"Yeah, I was just thinking that I'm starved," answered Mighty Boy. "I can't wait for lunch. I hope Bob and Derek have something good."

"Yeah," agreed Howard. "Me, too."

They climbed carefully down the rocks. Mighty Boy faced Howard. His hands were on his hips.

"Okay. Where to?"

"What?" asked Howard.

"Which way do we go?" said Mighty Boy.

Howard stared at him for a moment, not understanding. Then Howard's eyes widened, and he slapped his cheeks.

"Oh, no! The blue markers!" he cried. "We forgot all about them!"

Howard couldn't believe it; how could he have been so careless? His father had drummed into him how important it was to stay on trails when you go hiking. Howard had been so excited to be with Mighty Boy, it had just slipped his mind. He looked around; there were no markers on any of the trees. Howard realized that he hadn't seen one since they ran toward the waterfall.

"What?" asked Mighty Boy. "Blue markers? Oh, yeah."

"We have to find them," urged Howard. "We have to retrace our steps from the waterfall."

"Okay," said Mighty Boy. "It's not a big deal. Let's just go back the way we came."

They started back in the direction they had come from. At least it seemed to be the direction they had come from. After walking for a while, they passed a rotting log. Mighty Boy was sure they'd passed it before. Howard didn't remember it but he didn't say anything. He probably just hadn't noticed it. He was with Mighty Boy, after all, and Mighty Boy knew more than he did.

They continued on, Howard noting that his shadow was getting a bit longer in front of him. It was probably around one o'clock now. He wondered if Bob and Derek were getting worried.

The forest was darker here and more dense. They hadn't passed a single blue marker. Howard's stomach was hurting a little now. Glancing at Mighty Boy, though, he felt better: Mighty Boy was walking fast and seemed very sure of where he was going. Of course Howard should have been paying attention earlier but he was lucky—at least Mighty Boy would never get lost in a forest.

They tromped past mushrooms: huge yellow ones and tiny pinkish ones. Normally Howard would stop to examine them, but not now. He watched as Mighty Boy stomped on a yellow mushroom as he pushed a branch out of his way. Howard, looking down at the smashed mushroom, got smacked in the head with the branch. Then he was jerked to a standstill: his backpack had gotten hooked on another one. He stopped to untangle it. Mighty Boy was now quite a bit ahead of him; Howard ran to catch up.

Howard was getting more and more worried. Nothing looked familiar to him. Even though he had messed up by going off the trail and hadn't looked for the markers before, he knew that he didn't recognize anything around him. He thought they should have come to the path already; it didn't seem as though they had run that far to get to the waterfall.

"Uh . . . MB?" Howard piped up timidly.

Mighty Boy stopped and turned around. "What?" His voice sounded irritated.

"I . . . I don't think this is the right way."

"Yes it is," Mighty Boy snapped. "*I* know where we are."

Howard didn't say anything.

They walked on farther, crossing a small patch of blue wildflowers. Howard knew they hadn't passed the wildflowers before, but he wasn't going to mention it. Mighty Boy seemed angry. The sun was hot on Howard's neck, and insects were buzzing around his head. His mouth was parched. Dodging a rotten stump, he saw that Mighty Boy had stopped ahead of him. Howard jogged over.

"Why did you stop?"

Mighty Boy didn't answer.

"What's wrong?" Howard persisted.

Mighty Boy still didn't answer. He turned away from Howard, cupped his hands to his mouth, and shouted, "Bob! Derek! Where are you guys?"

Howard was surprised. "Wha—?"

"Hey, guys!" Mighty Boy continued. "Bob! Derek!"

There was no answer.

Howard cleared his throat. "Uh, MB, why . . . ?"

Turning his back and completely ignoring Howard, Mighty Boy began to walk in a big circle, shouting in every direction.

"BOB! DEREK! CAN YOU HEAR ME? BOB! DEREK!"

There was no response.

"HELLOOOO! BOB! DEREK! ANYBODY?"

The words echoed in the quiet.

Suddenly Mighty Boy picked up a large branch and hurled it forcefully away. Frozen, Howard just watched. His heart was beating fast.

Mighty Boy walked over to a fallen tree and got on top of it. "GUYS! ANYONE! CAN ANY-ONE HEAR ME?"

There was nothing but silence.

Sitting down on the log, Mighty Boy took a deep breath and stared at the ground. Howard took a step toward him, but the look on Mighty Boy's face stopped him. Mighty Boy jumped up onto the log again.

"HELP! SOMEBODY! ANYBODY! HELP!"

Mighty Boy's voice was raw and hoarse. He listened for a second and then sank back down, as if his legs weren't strong enough to support him. Mighty Boy hung his head low and uttered two words.

"Oh, no."

It was completely quiet for a few seconds. Howard could hear the blood pulsating in his ears. He took another step toward Mighty Boy. Hearing him, Mighty Boy jerked his head up. They stared at each other for an instant, then suddenly Mighty Boy bolted into the woods.

Stunned, Howard gazed at the figure getting smaller and smaller through the trees. Then he began to run.

"Wait!"

Howard took off after Mighty Boy at top speed. He didn't think that he'd ever run so far or so fast in his life. He had to catch him. When he was close enough, he leaped onto Mighty Boy's cape and the two of them fell to the ground.

"Wh-wh-"—Howard was panting so hard he could barely speak—"What's going on?"

Mighty Boy sat up, grabbed his cape back, and looked away. But Howard caught a glimpse of his face. And what he saw on it was something he'd never seen before, not even when Mighty Boy was cornered by the World Federation of United Supervillains: he saw fear.

"What's—?"

"What's going on? Going on! What do you think?" shouted Mighty Boy. "We're lost. That's what's going on. I have no idea where we are."

"Lost?" Howard echoed. He was baffled. "How can we be lost? You just said we were going the right way."

Mighty Boy looked away. "I didn't know which was the right way."

"Wait a minute." Howard started talking fast. "You *can* figure out the way we're supposed to go. Remember when Plantazoid made all the plants in the world carnivorous, so they ate animals and people? The jade plant in your living room grew fangs and ate your sister's hamster. The bonsai next door attacked the mailman. You tracked Plantazoid down to her underground greenhouse. Near the Mighty Cave you and Ouka found buried primal plant leaves, which told you how to unlock the deepest secrets of the forests, the timeless wisdom of the stones, the many wonders of the mountains. *You're*—"

"I'm not Mighty Boy, you idiot! Can't you get

that through your brain?" Mighty Boy was towering over him now. "I'm just a kid who plays him on TV! I don't have superpowers!"

Howard stared up at him.

"You still don't get it?" Mighty Boy shouted. "It's a show, it's imaginary, it's fake. . . . *It's all made up!* I *don't* know the way out of here. I have no idea where we are. We're lost. We'll probably never get out."

Howard was blinking now. "But . . . but you know about nature," he said weakly. "Don't you?"

"No!" Mighty Boy snapped. "I know *nothing* about nature. I hate nature!"

Howard was dumbfounded. He felt like he'd just been kicked hard in the stomach. This couldn't be right. What was Mighty Boy saying? He doesn't have superpowers. He's just a kid who plays Mighty Boy on TV. It's all made up?

Of course it's all made up. Howard had known *that*.

He stood up, leaned against a tree, and closed his eyes.

Or had he?

Part of him had known it.

But part of him hadn't. Part of him hadn't *wanted* to know it.

Howard turned and glared at Mighty Boy, who was now pacing back and forth. Howard wanted to run over and punch Mighty Boy in the nose or push him down and kick him hard in the side. The thought almost made him laugh out loud. *Howard Weinstein kicking Mighty Boy?*

But then the laugh caught in his throat.

And choked him up.

And Howard finally *knew* that . . . he was with a kid who just played Mighty Boy on TV.

Howard was sitting on a rock, hugging his knees and staring out into the woods. Mighty Boy sat hunched over on a log, his chin resting on his hands. They'd been that way for a while.

Mighty Boy spoke up dejectedly. "So now what should we do? We just roam around?"

Howard shrugged his shoulders. He didn't know or care. He turned his head, wiping his face so that Mighty Boy wouldn't see. He felt like he'd been in these woods for a month.

Mighty Boy stood up. "Well, I'm going to get out of here."

Howard didn't say anything. Mighty Boy was looking at him, waiting for him to get up. Howard turned his head and looked away again.

Mighty Boy paused and then started off slowly. Howard picked up a stick and started to pull off the bark. He felt angry and sad and embarrassed all at the same time. He didn't care what happened to him *or* Mighty Boy anymore.

But then he heard a sound. A strange sound. He stopped pulling at the bark and listened closely. After a few seconds he heard it again, more clearly this time.

"Aaaah . . ."

The hairs on the back of Howard's neck stood up. There was something wrong.

Something very wrong.

"Haaah . . . "

This time he knew what it was. It was someone trying to say something, but the words were stuck in their throat. Just like when Howard had tried to scream in the closet under the *Mighty Boy* set and nothing had come out. Howard took some steps forward, looking for Mighty Boy.

He spotted him a little way ahead, the red cape bright in the forest.

Howard began to run. He was about three feet from Mighty Boy when he opened his mouth to say something. But then he stopped dead in his tracks.

Directly in front of Mighty Boy, poking around the base of a tree, was a black bear. "Haaa . . . " Mighty Boy's voice was a gargle. Howard knew he was trying to say his name.

"Don't move a muscle," Howard whispered behind him. "Stand absolutely still."

The bear, eating some berries, looked up now and then at Mighty Boy.

"The bear's just looking for food," said Howard, trying to keep his voice steady. "We don't have any."

"B-b-but aren't *w-w-we* food to a bear?"

"No," answered Howard. "He's looking for easier food."

"H-how do y-you know?"

"Because this happened once to me and my dad," Howard replied. "Now start moving backward, very, very slowly."

Mighty Boy took a step back. The bear suddenly looked hard at him. Mighty Boy gasped.

"It's okay," Howard said softly. "Stay calm. You have to try not to panic. Animals can smell panic."

Mighty Boy took another step back. Howard could hear his breathing.

"That's good. Keep going."

Howard looked at the bear. He'd never seen one this close-up before. It would've been kind of cute if it had been in a zoo, safely behind some bars. He could tell that it was a youngish bear— older than a cub, but not full-grown yet. He wondered if its mother was nearby. They'd have to run as soon as they had a chance.

Mighty Boy had almost reached Howard.

"One more step," he said to him. "C'mon."

Mighty Boy took another step back; the bear took a step away from the tree. Mighty Boy let out a cry, tripped over a small log, and fell backward. The bear took a step toward them. Mighty Boy scrambled around on the ground.

"Oh no, oh no," he whimpered. "We're going to die. This is it. Help!"

Slowly Howard knelt down and clamped his hand on Mighty Boy's shoulder. "Be quiet."

"But . . . but . . . but—"

"Stand up as slowly and quietly as you can. Now."

The bear was watching them. Then it took a step closer. Mighty Boy, standing now, whimpered but didn't move. Howard was terrified, too, but he knew he couldn't show it. Then the bear began to open its mouth.

"Oh no," cried Mighty Boy softly. "It's going to eat us!"

The bear was yawning. As soon as Howard realized it, he grabbed Mighty Boy's arm and took off at high speed. He didn't know if it was the smartest thing to do, but it seemed right. He let go of Mighty Boy and kept running as fast and as hard as he could. Glancing back, there didn't seem to be any sign of the bear. He kept going just to be safe.

"W-w-wait!" gasped Mighty Boy.

Howard stopped and turned around.

Mighty Boy was bent over, his arms clutching his stomach, panting hard. "I . . . can't . . . run . . . that . . . fast. My stomach hurts. I have to stop for a second."

Howard was surprised at how far behind Mighty Boy was. He looked around and listened closely. There was nothing following them. He let out a sigh of relief and wiped his forehead with his sleeve. Leaning against a tree, he felt better.

Until he realized that they now were even deeper in the woods.

More lost than ever.

10

"I couldn't believe it when I saw that bear right in front of me," said Mighty Boy.

"I thought I was going to jump out of my skin. I've never been so scared in my life."

Howard didn't reply. His brain was churning. Running from the bear had shaken him into alertness. Now he remembered more of the things his dad had told him during their trips in the woods. The first thing to do if you're lost, Howard recalled, is to stop. They'd already messed that up because of the bear. But they probably shouldn't go any farther than they needed to.

"Now what should we do?" asked Mighty Boy.

Howard looked up at the sky, comparing the sun's position with what it had been the last time he checked. He thought it had been around one o'clock then. He noticed his shadow was longer now, too, so he guessed it was about two o'clock.

"I think we should find a spot for the night and then stay put," said Howard.

Mighty Boy stared at him. "*For the night? Are you joking?*"

Howard shook his head.

"I can't stay here overnight. I don't have anything to sleep on."

But Howard didn't listen to him; he had too much on his mind. They had to find a place to stay overnight, but they shouldn't go farther into the forest. Howard told Mighty Boy to wait a moment while he checked out the immediate area. Mighty Boy, who was still protesting, suddenly looked worried.

"Where are you going?" he asked. "I'm not staying here alone."

"It's just for a second," Howard assured him. "I just need to see what's around."

"But . . ." Mighty Boy said, biting his lip.

"I'll be right back," said Howard and started off.

Howard made his way through some tall bushes. He didn't see much except trees, trees, and more trees—none of them with blue markers. He climbed on top of a log and gazed out, finally spotting what appeared to be a small clearing near some pine trees. It would be a good place to spend the night. He went back to get Mighty Boy.

"I found a good place," said Howard.

"A good place for what?"

"To stay overnight," Howard explained.

"But . . . but . . ." Mighty Boy stammered.

"Come on," Howard replied firmly.

Howard moved quickly. Mighty Boy hurried behind him.

When they reached the clearing, Howard looked around, making a mental note of everything he could see. In front of him was a slope; he couldn't make out what was at the bottom. To his left were some big boulders—four of them, Howard counted. To the right was a rotted stump covered with moss and mushrooms. And next to that were several pine trees; Howard walked over to them to have a closer look. He leaned down and patted the bed of amber-colored needles.

"We're lucky," he remarked. "These are great to sleep on."

Mighty Boy didn't look like he felt lucky. He looked miserable. "Aren't they kind of sharp? Ouch!" He smacked his neck. "Darned thing bit right through my shirt. This stupid costume can't even protect me from a mosquito."

That reminded Howard of the next thing they had to do. "We have to make a fire. If we don't, we'll get eaten alive after the sun goes down."

"What will eat us alive?" asked Mighty Boy, turning pale. "Bears?"

"No," Howard replied. "Mosquitoes."

"And how are we supposed to make a fire?" Mighty Boy asked. "I don't have any matches."

Howard didn't answer; he was walking around, staring down at the ground. Mighty Boy sighed and sat down on the pine needles. "Ouch! They're sharp!

"What are you looking for?" he asked then, watching Howard. Suddenly he perked up. "I know. Two sticks, right? That's how to make a fire!" He picked up two small twigs and started to rub them together. "Is this right?"

"Uh, that really doesn't work," Howard said. "My dad says the only way to start a fire without matches is with special kinds of rocks. They're called flint and they have sparkles in them. Like this." He held up a gray rock with stripes. "Find more of these, and then we'll hit them together and make a spark."

Mighty Boy and Howard found a lot of the sparkly rocks. They hit them together over and over, but nothing happened. Finally, Mighty Boy threw down the ones he was holding. "This doesn't work. I'm sick of trying."

Howard put his down too. "It's a lot harder to do this than I thought. I wonder if I remembered how to do it right. . . ."

Mighty Boy hit his neck again. "Ouch! I wish Dr. Burn were here."

Howard looked at him sharply. "But he's made-up, an imaginary character."

"I know, I know." Mighty Boy smiled slyly at him. "I was just checking."

Howard smiled in spite of himself. Dr. Burn was actually Dr. Bernard Burnstein, a mild-mannered chemist at the local university. He was combining toxic chemicals one day when they spilled and caught fire in his laboratory. Part of Dr. Burnstein's head got burned. It turned out that the chemicals had seeped into his brain and created an evil personality, Dr. Burn. Dr. Burn *needed* to light fires and destroy everything around him, and he could take possession of nice Dr. Burnstein at any time.

"Yeah, that was a good episode," Howard reflected. "I liked it at the end when Mighty Boy— uh, I mean, *you*—were closing in on him, and he ran out of his lab into the parking lot. He wanted to set fire to the chemistry building but didn't have any matches, so he—"

Howard stopped. He and Mighty Boy stared at each other.

"He used his glasses!" they exclaimed in unison.

Howard whipped off his glasses and balanced them over a few branches. Sunlight glinted off the glass; he hoped the sun was still strong enough. But what was actually supposed to happen? When Dr. Burn did it, everything exploded into flames.

Mighty Boy watched Howard work. "Gee, I wish I could remember more. I wasn't even in that scene."

Howard felt the branches; they were getting warm, but that was all. There had to be something important he was forgetting, but what? He closed his eyes and tried to think hard about what his dad would do. While he was doing this, Mighty Boy started to pace, crunching dry leaves as he moved. Howard opened his eyes.

"That's it! We need to crumple up stuff *under* the glasses. Something that will catch a spark, like dead leaves or . . . or . . . paper!" He pulled off his backpack. "They put paper in here so it would look full. This is perfect."

He quickly opened the pack, took out the crumpled newspaper, and arranged it in a pile. Holding his glasses about six inches above, he began moving them slightly, back and forth. The sunlight, focused through the glass, created a tiny, white-hot spot on the paper.

"Hurry and gather as many small twigs and branches as you can," Howard instructed. "Don't pull any off the trees; they're too green. Just get the dry ones on the ground. A lot of them."

Mighty Boy headed off. After a few minutes he was back, dragging a huge log.

"Look! All we need is this."

Howard was surprised that Mighty Boy didn't know better. "No, that's way too big. We have no way to cut it. We need small dead branches and twigs—hurry!"

Mighty Boy took off, returning this time with an armload of twigs and branches. He crouched down next to Howard, who was carefully laying dry leaves under the newspaper. "Look!" Mighty Boy cried. "It's starting!"

The tiny spot on the paper had become a spark, which was growing bigger and bigger. Howard took his glasses away and started to blow; he could see some very small flames.

"Wow! That's amazing!" Mighty Boy looked awed. "I can't believe you did it."

Howard smiled. "For once I'm glad I wear glasses."

"They're a lot more useful than fake laser vision," added Mighty Boy.

"Now we have to get lots and lots of wood—as much as we can carry."

Howard showed Mighty Boy the size sticks that would help the flames grow. Anything too big could put them out, he explained; he'd done that himself once with his dad. They took turns collecting wood and fanning the fire. Howard was break-

"Okay," said Mighty Boy shakily.

Howard took off his glasses and wiped his face. Mighty Boy was just like Howard the first time his father had taken him camping. Now he knew how scared his father had felt when Howard tried to eat those berries. He took a deep breath; that had been close.

Howard wrinkled his nose and took another deep breath. This time he smelled something— something he hadn't noticed before. It was water.

"You know what?" He turned to Mighty Boy. "I think there's a lake or pond around here."

"Where?" asked Mighty Boy.

"I'm not sure. But it's close by, I think," he answered. "Let's go back and feed the fire before we look. That way the smoke will lead us back to our campsite."

After piling the fire high with branches and checking to be sure it would burn safely, they walked back to where the deadly nightshade grew. Howard could make out some smaller trees and a clearing a short distance away. They headed over to the clearing and soon found themselves on the shore of a small lake. Howard turned to check their campsite; he could see a small stream of smoke. By the looks of his long shadow in front of him, he figured it was now about four o'clock. The fire was southwest of where they now stood, according to the sun.

Mighty Boy was crouched on the shore, cupping his hands into the water. "Jeez, I'm so thirsty."

"Don't drink from it!" Howard exclaimed.

Mighty Boy looked up at him, disappointed. "Why not?"

"Lakes have lots of bacteria in them. You might get sick."

"You can't do anything in the woods!" pouted Mighty Boy.

"You can if you know what's safe," replied Howard. Even though he knew more than Mighty Boy, there was plenty he didn't know. There were also plenty of ways to get hurt, he knew.

Mighty Boy was leaning over, watching the water intently. Suddenly he shot his arm out to grab something. He lost his balance and toppled into the lake headfirst.

Howard started laughing.

Mighty Boy sat up, wiping his face. "There's lots of fish in here. I tried to catch one."

"They're probably lake trout," said Howard. "My dad and I cook them sometimes on our camping trips. They're good when you're really hungry."

"You mean like now?" Mighty Boy tried to grab one again.

"You're never going to catch it that way," Howard remarked.

Mighty Boy stood up and squeezed the water out of his cape. His hair was plastered down on his forehead and the red MB letters on his chest were hanging off. He took off a slipper and held it upside down. A stream of brown water poured out.

Howard imagined Mighty Boy looking this way as he got ready to karate-kick a supervillain and couldn't help giggling. He looked pretty . . . unmighty.

Mighty Boy giggled, too, and threw his slipper at Howard. "Quit laughing at me. What's *your* bright idea to catch a fish?"

Howard walked over to a large rock, rolled it, then picked up something brown and slimy.

"Ee-yew. Gross. What is that?"

"A slug," Howard answered. "Perfect bait."

He crouched down and dipped part of the slug into the water, waiting to see if a fish might take a nibble. Nothing happened. "I need a fishing line," he said, looking around on the ground.

Mighty Boy picked up a long stick. "Here. Put the slug on the end of it and see what happens."

Howard put the rolled-up slug on the end of the branch and held it over the water. It fell off. He got up, rolled the large rock again, and found another slug. But when he stood up, the slug slipped through his fingers and landed on his sneaker. Howard stared at his shoe—an idea popped into his head. Howard yanked at his shoelace, pulling it out in one quick motion. He'd found a fishing line.

He laid the slug down on the boulder and cinched his shoelace around it.

"Ta-da! A fishing line!"

The slug fell out of the shoelace.

"We need something to poke through the slug that will hold it like a hook," said Howard. He took off his glasses and looked at the little screw that held the sides together. No, that wouldn't work. He wedged his hands into his pockets. Nothing.

Mighty Boy, watching him, said, "This stupid costume doesn't have any pockets, so I know I don't have anything."

The boys sat down on the shore and looked out at the water. Howard was disappointed; the shoelace had been such a good idea.

"Hey, wait a minute!" Mighty Boy jumped up. "I have a pin, a safety pin. We had to pin my cape to my suit because it wasn't staying on."

Howard pulled down the back of Mighty Boy's cape. Sure enough, there were three safety pins.

"Hooray!" Howard cheered. He picked up the slug in one hand, a pin in the other. "You're going to stick that through the slug?" Mighty Boy asked.

Howard nodded.

"Yuck. I don't think I can watch. Tell me when you're done." Mighty Boy turned around.

Howard laughed as he pushed the pin through. "Done." Then he tied the shoelace to the pin. He moved as close as he could to the water, put his arm out, and hung the shoelace down. The slug was submerged. They waited. Nothing happened. After a few minutes Howard put his arm down.

"Whew. It's hard to hold your arm out for a long time."

Mighty Boy nodded. "Let me try."

Howard glanced back at the fire; the smoke was dwindling. He couldn't let it go out.

"I need to run back for a second and feed the fire," Howard said.

"Go ahead," said Mighty Boy. "I promise I won't go in very far."

Howard headed back, picking up as much firewood as he could carry on the way. The flame was small, so he put two larger logs on either side and stacked a couple of medium-sized branches on top. Then he knelt down and puffed on the fire. The flames got bigger. The boys would need a lot more wood if they wanted their fire to last for even part of the night. Howard gathered more, losing track of the time, until he heard Mighty Boy.

"Howard! Howard!"

He'd forgotten about him! Howard's heart started to pound. He threw down his pile of sticks and ran. What if Mighty Boy had waded too far into the lake? What if he couldn't swim? Howard ran as fast as he could to the lake. Mighty Boy was nowhere to be seen. Howard felt a sick feeling in his stomach.

"MB? MB! Where are you?"

"Right here," he answered, standing up a couple of yards down the shore from Howard. He held up his arm proudly. "Look!"

At the end of Howard's shoelace hung a big, beautiful lake trout, about sixteen inches long.

"Wow! I've never seen one that big!" yelled Howard. "That's incredible!"

Mighty Boy was beaming. "Can you believe it?" He lifted the long fish up higher and gazed at it in wonder. "I caught my first fish!"

12

Howard looked at Mighty Boy, who was struggling to hold the wriggling fish, and took a deep breath. "Okay, now we've got to gut the fish."

Mighty Boy looked puzzled. "What's 'gut'?"

"Take its insides out," said Howard.

Mighty Boy looked horrified. "That's disgusting! I'm not doing that."

"It's not so bad once you do it a few times. Besides, you can't eat the insides of fish. Some parts are poisonous," Howard explained.

Mighty Boy looked down sadly at the fish. "You take the insides out when it's alive? That seems . . . kind of painful."

"No, you kill it first," replied Howard. "My dad showed me how to do it . . . humanely."

Mighty Boy had a sick look on his face. "First the pin in the slug, and now this. . . . "

"I'll let you know when I'm done," Howard said, taking the fish from Mighty Boy.

Howard walked a little way and turned around. Mighty Boy was sitting down on the ground, cringing. He had his fingers in his ears. Howard covered his mouth so that he wouldn't laugh.

He whacked the fish once against a large rock.

Then he looked through some sticks, found the one he needed, and peeled back the bark on one end to make it sharper. He laid the fish down and made a neat, straight slice down its soft belly. Then, inserting a few fingers inside the slice, he scooped everything out in a sweeping motion.

Howard went to the lake and squatted down, washing the blood off the fish. He poked one little hole in the fish's tail and another one near its head so that he could run a branch through the length of its body. This way they could hold it over the fire.

He headed back to Mighty Boy.

"Did you . . . do it?" asked Mighty Boy when he saw Howard.

Howard nodded. "It's time for barbecued lake trout."

The boys went back to the campsite. Howard showed Mighty Boy how to hold the fish over the fire, turning it gently to cook it evenly.

"That eye staring up at me gives me the creeps," said Mighty Boy.

"Don't look at it," Howard told him, smiling. He could remember his father saying the exact same thing to him the first time they caught a fish and cooked it themselves. The fish began to smell delicious; it was finally ready. They devoured it in about fifteen seconds.

"Mmm, that was so good," said Mighty Boy. "I

can't believe it's gone already. I didn't even care that it had bones."

"I could've eaten about four whole fish," Howard chimed in.

"Wait until I tell my mom that I'd rather have lake trout than a Jumbo-burger," Mighty Boy said, leaning back and patting his stomach. "She'll wonder if I've been replaced by a replicant or a zombie doll."

Howard laughed as he got up. "I'm going to bury these bones so animals won't smell them."

Howard dug up some dirt on the far side of the pine trees. He noticed that his shadow was quite long and that the sun was beginning to set. It was probably about six-thirty or seven. When he got back, Mighty Boy was hovering close to the fire; the temperature was dropping fast.

"I'm sure glad that you knew to get lots of wood to burn," Mighty Boy said, shivering. "You know, if I were out here by myself, I would've: one, got eaten by a bear; two, been attacked by carnivorous mosquitoes; three, poisoned myself with berries; four, starved; and five, froze."

Howard laughed.

"You sure know a lot about the outdoors," Mighty Boy went on. "Your dad must be a good teacher."

"He is," agreed Howard as he threw some branches onto the fire.

It was quiet for a little while. For the first time Howard thought about his parents and how worried they must be. He felt bad and hoped his dad realized how much he'd taught Howard.

Then Mighty Boy sighed. "I don't know very much about anything."

Howard looked at him, surprised. "What do you mean? You're on television. You know about lots of things."

"Like what?"

"Well . . . " Howard paused, thinking. "You know how to memorize lines. You have that special kind of memory, right?"

"I guess so." Mighty Boy shrugged. "But they also write the lines on big poster boards and hold them up near the scenes just in case I need them." He sighed. "I usually do."

The light from the fire made Mighty Boy's costume look shiny. His stomach muscles looked powerful.

"Well, what about those stomach muscles? I sure don't have *those*."

"Give me a hard punch in the stomach," said Mighty Boy, moving over.

Howard punched him. Mighty Boy's stomach felt rock hard.

"No, punch harder than that," urged Mighty Boy. "As hard as you can. You won't hurt me, really."

Howard reared back and punched hard.

"Ouch! That hurt my hand," said Howard.

Mighty Boy laughed. "That's because they're plastic! Built right into the costume." He lifted the material from his stomach, and all the stomach muscles went with it. Then he pulled his plastic right-arm muscle up. "Here too." Mighty Boy's regular arm below looked skinny. Maybe even as skinny as Howard's.

Howard smiled. He should've guessed.

"Okay, but what about karate? Your coach said you were pretty good, right?"

"Well, alright," Mighty Boy conceded. "I'm getting pretty good at karate. It's the only real thing I get to do on the show. Everything else is either special effects or just plain fake, like these muscles or stuffed Ouka."

"That sounds like a dish my mother would make in her cooking class," remarked Howard.

They both laughed. Howard gazed at the fire and breathed a contented sigh. He'd forgotten the sounds and smells of the forest at night. The world seemed small and cozy right now, as if he and Mighty Boy were the only two people on earth.

After a little while Howard showed Mighty Boy how to make a bed of crossed branches and pine needles.

Mighty Boy stretched out on his bed. "Wow, this *is* comfortable. And it smells great."

They lay down on their pine beds and watched the fire.

"What's all that hissing noise?" asked Mighty Boy.

"That's chirping. Crickets and katydids do it. They chirp at night when they're looking for mates. They're really loud out here."

"They sure are."

"Look." Howard pointed to a cluster of fireflies. "Aren't those neat?"

"Cool!" said Mighty Boy. "I don't think I've ever seen so many fireflies all together."

"When you get home, get a jar and collect some for a night. I did that once and put them on my nightstand," said Howard. "They lit up my whole room."

"Great idea."

The boys watched—and listened—to the night insects in silence for a while. Finally Mighty Boy broke the quiet. "Do you think we'll find our way out of here tomorrow?"

Howard turned on his side and propped himself up on one elbow. "People will be looking for us. They might be looking right now."

"Do you think they'll find us?"

Howard nodded and added, "Definitely." He hadn't really felt that certain but, strangely enough, after he said it he did.

The fire hissed and crackled loudly.

Mighty Boy curled into a ball on his bed. "Brrr! It's cold out here. I've never spent the night outside before."

Howard sat up and looked at him. "Are you kidding?"

Mighty Boy shook his head.

"You've never gone camping with your dad?"

Mighty Boy shook his head again.

"Not even in the backyard?"

"Nope," he answered. "We're really busy all the time with the show. And besides, there's no room in our yard because of the swimming pool."

"Wow." Howard couldn't believe it. He couldn't imagine life without camping. "Going camping with my dad is my favorite thing to do in the whole world. It's the greatest."

After a few seconds Mighty Boy asked, "So you learned *all* this stuff from your dad?"

Howard nodded. "Yeah. I never really thought it was learning stuff. We just did it."

"After we get back, maybe I could go camping with you and your dad," suggested Mighty Boy.

Howard grinned. "Sure! That would be great."

Mighty Boy picked up an acorn and threw it into the fire. "My dad works in the studio's accounting office. Both he and my mom quit their other jobs to manage my career." Mighty Boy sounded sad.

"Oh." Howard wasn't sure what to say.

"Sometimes I don't even know if I *like* having a career," said Mighty Boy. "I don't have friends or go to school or do any of the stuff normal kids do."

"But what about the kids who play your friends on the show? Aren't they your friends?" asked Howard.

Mighty Boy snorted. "No. They just *play* my friends. Most of them are mad because they don't get to be Mighty Boy, even though they know it's all fake. They act really snotty. Nobody acts like a real kid." He paused. "Like this."

Howard put his arms under his head and leaned back. Mighty Boy leaned back next to him.

"Wow!" exclaimed Mighty Boy. "Look at all the stars! I've never seen so many. The sky looks enormous."

"Yep." Howard remembered how special it was when he saw the stars like this for the first time. "Look," he said. "There's the Big Dipper. See it? And the North Star."

"Where?"

Howard showed him. He pointed out which stars were planets too.

They gazed up at the sky. Howard suddenly felt exhausted. He closed his eyes and was just about to fall asleep when Mighty Boy spoke again.

"None of those kids I work with even know my real name."

Howard didn't say anything for a minute.

Incredibly, it had never occurred to him that Mighty Boy *had* a real name, except for Michael Boyer.

"Wait a minute. What about *MB*?" asked Howard.

"That's not my real name. It's just a nick-name."

"Oh," said Howard.

Mighty Boy sat up. "It's not that I want every-one to start calling me by my real name; I'd just like someone to *know* it. Friends know each other's real names even if the whole world calls them by their nicknames. You know what I mean?"

Howard nodded. "So . . . what is your real name?"

Mighty Boy took a deep breath. "Seymour."

"Seymour?" For a minute Howard thought he was joking but when he saw his face, he knew he wasn't.

"Well," Howard said. "*Howard*'s not much better."

Mighty Boy laughed. "I guess not."

Howard thought about the fire. He figured that it would probably go out sometime during the night, but he wanted to make it last as long as possible. He got some big branches and threw them on top. Then he lay back down. Mighty Boy unpinned his cape and covered them both up.

They were quiet for a while. Howard could tell that Mighty Boy was going to speak up, but he had something to say first. He cleared his throat.

"Don't worry. I won't tell anyone about your name . . . Seymour."

Mighty Boy smiled at him. "Thanks. I was just about to ask you that."

"Good-night."

"Good-night."

13

The birds were making a racket. Howard opened his eyes. Staring at the sky, he didn't know where he was for a second; then he saw the cape and Mighty Boy sleeping next to him. Mighty Boy opened his eyes a few minutes later.

"Hi," he said, yawning. "Well, we made it."

"Yep. That bear didn't find us," said Howard.

Mighty Boy huddled under his cape. "Brrr! It's freezing. Let's make another fire."

"We can't yet," said Howard. "The sun isn't strong enough. I think we should hike for a while and try to find our way back."

Mighty Boy got up and wrapped his cape around himself. "Okay. You're the expert. Point me in the right direction."

Howard started off, heading away from the slope and the lake. Remembering that the sun had been slightly behind him when they left the set the day before, Howard thought they should go east. Dew sparkled on the leaves and bushes; the forest smelled fresh. Sunlight filtered through the trees, lighting dust particles that floated through the air. So far Howard didn't recognize anything. He wondered if he'd gotten too confused to find his way.

Howard was worried. What if he was getting them even more lost? He felt tired and hungry and decided that he'd had enough of this adventure. He was ready to go home—to his new home. He closed his eyes and imagined his kitchen; it seemed like the most wonderful place on earth. His mom and dad were probably eating breakfast right now, having something icky like an asparagus omelette. But he'd be eating warm waffles with melted butter and maple syrup, with a tall glass of orange juice to drink.

Lost in his daydream, it took Howard a little while to realize that something felt strange on his feet. His shoes were wet. He stopped and looked around; there wasn't any water that he could see. Then he saw a spot where the leaves looked darker; he went over and crouched down. It was a small spring, bubbling up from the ground.

"Mighty Boy," Howard called.

Up ahead a little way, Mighty Boy turned around. Howard motioned for him to come over. They crouched down.

"It's a freshwater spring," explained Howard. "We can finally have a drink."

They cupped their hands, filled them, and

drank over and over again. Mighty Boy dumped some water on his head, rubbing his face vigorously. Then he stopped and looked around.

"Doesn't this mean that there's more water somewhere around here?" he asked.

Howard nodded. "Yeah. But we're far from the lake. And there's nothing around."

"Maybe it's the—" began Mighty Boy.

Then Howard thought of it too. "The waterfall! Good thinking!"

They followed the damp leaves for a while, through a darker part of the woods, which Howard thought seemed familiar. He had bent down to tie his shoe when he heard a faint noise. He looked up and saw that Mighty Boy was concentrating hard on something. "It's the waterfall. Can you hear it?"

Howard could. "Yep!"

The boys headed in the direction of the waterfall. The sound of rushing water was getting louder and louder. Suddenly they heard dogs barking and people shouting. Before Howard knew it, they were in the middle of a large group, some of them park rangers with megaphones. They'd run right into their rescue team.

"They're here!" someone shouted.

Howard saw Derek and Bob and the other crew members.

"Howard! Mighty Boy!" Mr. Levine shouted. "Thank God we found you!"

Mr. Levine put his arms around both boys. "Are you all right? We were frantic. I've been on the phone with both of your parents all night."

Mighty Boy nodded. "Yeah, we're fine. Just hungry."

"Very hungry," Howard chimed in.

A big man in a dark-green ranger uniform shook his head. "Whew! You guys are lucky you didn't take a wrong turn and get even more lost. This forest is over a thousand acres."

More people were coming, Howard saw—a lot more. A man with a camera on his shoulder and a woman with a microphone were leading the pack. She stopped near them and tested her microphone to make sure it was working. Then she approached Mighty Boy.

"I'm from WPLR, Channel Five, and we'd like to do a live broadcast on the rescue, okay?"

Howard and Mighty Boy looked at each other. "Sure."

The woman put the microphone up to her lips and looked gravely at the camera.

"This is Tammy Talbot, live from Wintergreen Forest, reporting on the dramatic rescue of Mighty Boy, who got lost while shooting on location for his show."

"And Howard Weinstein," Mighty Boy piped up.

Tammy Talbot turned. "What? Oh, yes. He was with Herman Weinstein, another boy."

"*Howard* Weinstein," said Mighty Boy.

"Mighty Boy," Tammy Talbot asked, "can you tell us exactly what happened when you discovered that you were lost, alone in the forest, with barely a chance to get out?"

"Well," said Mighty Boy, "it really wasn't that bad because Howard knew what to do."

"What to do?" echoed Tammy Talbot. "Could you explain that in more detail, please?"

More reporters moved in; there were four microphones in Mighty Boy's face.

"Howard knew what to do when we saw a bear. He stopped me from eating poison berries." Mighty Boy paused for a moment. "In fact, Howard probably saved my life."

There was a loud gasp, and then all the reporters scrambled over to where Howard was standing. A bunch of microphones were thrust into Howard's face. He backed away and adjusted his glasses.

"Ladies and gentlemen," Tammy Talbot said urgently, "in a just-breaking story, Channel Five has learned that last night this courageous young boy, Howard Weinstein"—she pushed Howard in front of the cameras—"saved Mighty Boy's life. Please tell us about these dramatic developments."

"Did the bear just pounce on you?" asked a man with a Channel Six microphone.

"Was it ready to tear you limb from limb?"

"Was it ferocious-looking and foaming at the mouth?"

"What kind of bear was it?"

"Did you wrestle it to the ground?"

"Are you an animal wrestler?"

"Are you an animal trainer?"

"Do you go to the zoo?"

"Was Mighty Boy"—Tammy Talbot lowered her voice dramatically—"close to death?"

A hush fell over the crowd.

Howard felt a little silly and didn't know what to say.

"Well," he said, "I just told him to stand still. When I thought we could run for it, we . . . ran for it."

A din broke out as cameras clicked and whirred. Howard was practically trampled as more people surged toward him. It seemed like everybody was calling his name. He didn't know who to answer first.

"Howard! Over here!"

"Howard! A question, please!"

"Howard! This way!"

Tammy Talbot leaned in. "Howard, we are all . . . *overwhelmed* to hear of your act of bravery. Can you tell us now how you saved Mighty Boy from eating poison berries?"

"Did you need to give Mighty Boy mouth-to-mouth?"

"How do you know so much about poison berries?"

"Was he," a man asked, "almost gone?"

Howard shrugged. "No. It wasn't a big deal. Mighty Boy said he found some berries. I knew they were poisonous, so I told him to spit them out."

Tammy Talbot leaned in again. "Howard, can you tell us how, exactly, you knew that these were poisonous berries?"

"Well," Howard said, "they're called deadly nightshade and they grow on vines in the ground. They look like they'd be good to eat; I know because I almost tried one once. My dad stopped me and told me what was safe to eat in the forest."

The reporters were stunned.

"An animal expert *and* a berry expert!"

"What strength! What courage!"

"Herman Weinstein . . . a hero for our time."

Mighty Boy piped up again. "It's *Howard*, and he also made a fishing line out of his shoelace, and we caught a fish!"

"Omigod!" cried a man with a camera. "I can't believe my ears!"

"Plus, Howard knew how to make a fire," Mighty Boy continued. "If he didn't, we probably would've frozen to death or been eaten by mosquitoes."

"How did you do it, Howard? Matches? Lighter? That kind of thing?" asked a woman with a notebook.

"No," answered Howard. "I used my glasses."

More gasps from the reporters.

"I've never heard of such a thing!" said the woman with the notepad.

"An animal expert and a berry expert and a glasses expert!"

"What a kid!" cried someone else.

Howard looked at Mighty Boy, and they both started to laugh. Howard covered his mouth with his hand to make a straight face. "I just held my glasses over a pile of paper and leaves until they made a spark. But Mighty Boy remembered it from the Dr. Burn episode."

"Howard knows so much about the outdoors," Mighty Boy said to Mr. Levine. "He said that I could go camping with him and his dad so they can teach me."

"So," said Tammy Talbot, smiling at the camera. "Then Howard Weinstein is . . . the boy who saved Mighty Boy."

Suddenly everyone began to clap and cheer. Howard adjusted his glasses and looked down at his shoes. He felt like he might burst with happiness.

14

On Monday Howard was sitting on a tall stool in front of his class.

"How did you know what to do when you saw the bear?" asked Emily Browne, one of Maggie McDoren's friends who had never spoken to Howard before.

"I remembered what my dad told me: stand still and don't make any noise," Howard answered. "But it was really hard not to scream and run."

Everyone in the class laughed except Eddie, who snorted loudly and said, "That's just what a Mighty Wimp would do."

"Eddie, be quiet," Mrs. Fowler scolded. Howard pointed to George Wheeler, a boy who had always ignored him.

"Was it scary by yourselves at night?"

Howard nodded. "Yeah, it was a little scary. But we were so tired from walking that we fell asleep pretty quickly."

Eddie snorted again. "Oh, sure, Mighty Wimp. I'll bet you were hiding under Mighty Boy's cape the whole time, crying for your mommy."

Mrs. Fowler gave Eddie a warning, and several kids turned around to tell him to shut up. Howard tried to ignore him, but it was hard. Howard might have changed after all that happened, but Eddie hadn't. That morning on his way into school, Eddie had stopped him in the hallway. He'd started threatening Howard because Mrs. Fowler had called his parents about the math test. But then Mr. Bowman, the principal, walked by and told Howard how proud he was of him. Eddie ducked away, but he let Howard know that he wasn't finished with him.

After Howard had gotten home from Wintergreen Forest, the phone hadn't stopped ringing. *Mighty Boy*, Howard learned, was broadcast all over the country and had fans everywhere. Reporters from places like Mississippi and Alaska called him; they all knew about the boys getting lost and wanted to talk to Howard.

On the local news, all three networks broadcast the interviews with Howard and Mighty Boy in the forest. Howard and his parents watched bits and pieces of all of them. Someone even called saying he was a Hollywood agent and asked if Howard would be interested in starring in a series of his own called *Nature Boy*. Howard wasn't. If he became a television star then he would have to stop being a regular boy, and if he stopped being a regular boy he wouldn't be able to do all the things he knew how to do, which were the things the agent thought would make him good for the series. It sounded complicated when Howard explained it to his mother, but she understood.

Then this morning before he'd left for school, the newspaper arrived with a front-page story about him and Mighty Boy. There was a picture of them with their arms around each other's shoulders and a caption that read, "Two Mighty Boys." Howard looked at the picture for a long time. He didn't know if he believed it.

Now Mrs. Fowler was standing behind Howard at the front of the room; it was almost time to leave. "Howard will answer more questions tomorrow if we have time. He has also promised to explain how he navigated by the sky and how he used his glasses to start a fire."

The bell rang and Howard packed up. When he walked out of the room, several kids from his class and other classes were waiting in the hall to talk to him. Two girls even had the photo from the morning paper and asked him to autograph it. Howard felt a little embarrassed but signed the papers anyway. Then Maggie came up with Emily and asked if Howard wanted to come over tomorrow. Howard said sure. Not one person giggled.

He had to get home quickly because Mighty Boy had said he would stop by on his way to the airport. The cast was going to do some shows in California. They would reshoot the scene in Wintergreen Forest when they got back.

Cutting through the alleys was the fastest way home, but Howard wasn't going to risk it. To Eddie, Howard was still Mighty Wimp no matter what anyone else thought, and he was going to get back at him for telling Mrs. Fowler about the math test. Unfortunately, Howard reflected, knowing what to do in the woods didn't make him any bigger or taller now.

Trudging up the small hill behind the school, he stopped and looked around. He didn't see anyone. If he hurried, he could make it through the park in about eight minutes. Maybe he could even find a honeycomb in the dead tree near the sassafras to give to Mighty Boy. Taking a deep breath, he darted into the park.

He walked quickly but uneasily, wishing he'd asked Maggie to walk home with him. But then Eddie might chase them both and Maggie would see—just when she and the other kids at school were starting to like him—that Howard still had to run from Eddie, that nothing had changed after all. He passed the picnic tables and the small jungle gym, and caught a whiff of the sweet blossoms of the sassafras. Then he heard something and froze.

A high-pitched giggle.

Eddie stepped out from behind the slide, sucking on a blue Popsicle.

"Well, if it isn't the nature nerd."

Howard picked up his pace. He couldn't believe it. How had Eddie gotten here without Howard seeing him?

"So you think you're really tough now, huh?" Eddie sneered, stepping into Howard's path. "I know you're not. I know that you're the same little twerp who ratted on me to Mrs. Fowler."

Howard stared at Eddie, feeling the familiar nervousness in his stomach. That dread hadn't gone away, he realized; it had just been on vacation for a few days. Smirking at Howard, Eddie tossed the Popsicle stick over his shoulder. Howard watched it land near a big fallen branch. Then he got an idea. Was it too risky? Instead of stopping to answer that question, he suddenly swerved around Eddie, picked up the big branch, and took off.

Eddie yanked on his arm, but Howard shook him off. As he raced on, he heard Eddie's grunts behind him, getting closer. Howard's legs were aching, and he knew that Eddie could overtake him at any second—but he didn't have much farther to go. Whizzing past the sassafras tree, Howard stopped in front of the dead tree trunk. He caught a glimpse of Eddie's furious face. This was it. If this didn't work, Howard was in the worst trouble of his life.

Rearing back, Howard smacked the tree trunk with the branch as hard as he could. He hit it once, twice, three times. At that moment Eddie leaped for him, but Howard ducked under his arm and around the trunk.

For a moment he didn't hear anything. Oh no, he thought, it didn't work. He felt queasy with fear. Now Eddie would be madder than ever.

Then he heard the sound he was waiting for— a low buzzing.

"Yaaa! Bees!" Eddie's shriek was even more shrill than his giggle. "They're all around! Help!"

Howard turned and saw Eddie covering his head with his hands. There were about ten bees swarming around his face. Howard knew that the sugary smell of the Popsicle was attracting the bees even more.

"How did you—?" Eddie's voice was muffled through his hands.

"I can't tell you that. But I'll warn you that you'd better not bother me again," said Howard in a grave voice. "I can command other creatures of the forest to suddenly attack you."

"No! Call them off!" Eddie shouted.

Howard bit his lips to keep from smiling. "It's too late. All you can do is . . . *run.*"

Eddie took off in the opposite direction; the bees followed him.

Howard let out a deep sigh of relief. He didn't think he'd ever seen a more wonderful sight.

It was practically like topping Jelloid with mini marshmallows.

"AH HA HA!"

Deep within the forest, Rainiac's evil laughter echoed off the walls of his cave laboratory, piercing the silence.

Rainiac was laughing because he now saw on his video screen what he'd been waiting for: kindly old Ma Boyer walking out her back door to putter in her little vegetable garden. She stopped to put on her wide-brimmed straw hat and canvas work gloves. When she reached the small patch of dirt, she sifted through her gardening basket for her tools. She knelt down and, humming a little tune, opened a packet of zucchini seeds.

But then she glanced up at the sky. For some very strange reason, there seemed to be an overcast just above her zucchini seeds. She knitted her brows together.

Rainiac darted his eyes to the overhead clock in the corner.

"Thirty, twenty-nine, twenty-eight, twenty-seven—" piped up Gag, Rainiac's pet cockatoo.

"Do silent counting, birdbrain," shouted Rainiac.

"Do silent counting, birdbrain," repeated Gag.

Rainiac yanked at one of his tail feathers.

Gazing back at Ma Boyer, Rainiac smiled in anticipation. He'd situated his specially formulated bacteria-filled cloud above Ma Boyer because the person he really wanted was Mighty Boy. Whenever one of the Boyers was in danger (which seemed to happen a lot), Mighty Boy was always around to save them. Rainiac's smile deepened. He suspected it was because Mighty Boy was secretly Michael Boyer, their adopted son. After Rainiac captured Mighty Boy, he would hold a press conference and tell the world all about it. Depending on how much of the world was left after Rainiac got through with it.

"AH HA HA!"

Checking the clock (twenty-one, twenty, nineteen), Rainiac watched as Ma Boyer put out her hand, a baffled expression on her face.

It had started to rain . . . but it was raining only on her. In the Joneses' yard next-door, it was sunny and warm.

Rainiac leaped over to a giant weather map. "And today, we will have a high front over much of the region, with warm air and sunny skies. Better get out those swimsuits, you beach bums."

He turned around for an instant. "Except, what is this? A little cloud. Over Main Street? Over one house on Main Street? Over one yard, to be precise." He giggled softly. "So, weather watchers, it's fair conditions every-where except over Ma Boyer's yard, where it's going to rain bacteria!

"AH HA HA!" screeched Rainiac.

"AH HA HA!" screeched Gag.

Meanwhile, outside in the forest, Mighty Boy stopped to listen. His sonar hearing was pick-ing up something. It sounded like laughter. Evil laughter. From deep within the forest. He knew that it could come from only one person: Rainiac. And his annoying cockatoo, Gag. Mighty Boy felt a ray of hope: he was on the right track.

Mighty Boy dashed up a steep hill. He
scanned the area for a sign of Rainiac's lair.
By his reading of the sky, he knew Rainiac's
lair had to be to the west. On his way down he
passed a patch of delicious-looking red
berries. But Mighty Boy didn't stop, even
though his throat was parched. He knew those
were poisonous berries and that Rainiac had
planted them there to try to lure him into eating some. Rainiac would have to do better
than that to trick Mighty Boy.

As Mighty Boy approached a small pond, he
came upon a boy hiking.

"Greetings, hiker," said Mighty Boy. "Have
you seen a suspicious-looking man coming
through here?"

The hiker shook his head. "No, I didn't see
anything."

Mighty Boy glanced around the area, making certain that Rainiac wasn't lurking around,
waiting to spring a trap. "Be careful in these
woods."

The hiker nodded. "Good luck, Mighty Boy."

The hiker watched as Mighty Boy—his gold-
en hair glinting in the light, his red cape billow-

ing in the wind, his stomach muscles tensed and ready for action—leaped past him on his mission to seek out and destroy Rainiac.

And the young hiker knew that the world would be safe for mankind. . . .

⚡